Also by Vivek Shraya

God Loves Hair

What I LOVE about Being QUEER

She of the Mountains

even this page is white

The Boy & the Bindi

I'm Afraid of Men

Death Threat

THE SUBTWEET

THE SUBTWEET

A NOVEL

VIVEK SHRAYA

Published by ECW Press
665 Gerrard Street East
Toronto, Ontario, Canada M4M 1Y2
416-694-3348 / info@ecwpress.com

Editor for the Press: Jennifer Knoch
Cover design: Jessica Albert
Cover artwork © Manjit Thapp/manjitthapp.co.uk
Author photo: © Vanessa Heins

This is a work of fiction. Names, characters, places, and incidents either are the product of the author's imagination or are used fictitiously, and any resemblance to actual persons, living or dead, business establishments, events, or locales is entirely coincidental.

"Sadness Is a Blessing"
Words and Music by Lykke Li Zachrisson,
Bjorn Yttling and Rick Nowels Copyright (c)
2011 EMI Music Publishing Scandinavia AB and
R-Rated Music

All Rights on behalf of EMI Music Publishing
Scandinavia AB Administered by Sony/ATV
Music Publishing LLC, 424 Church Street,
Suite 1200, Nashville, TN 37219

All Rights on behalf of R-Rated Music
Administered by Universal Music Works
International Copyright Secured All Rights
Reserved

Reprinted by Permission of Hal Leonard LLC

LIBRARY AND ARCHIVES CANADA CATALOGUING
IN PUBLICATION

Title: The subtweet : a novel / Vivek Shraya.

Names: Shraya, Vivek, 1981– author.

Identifiers: Canadiana (print) 20190201517
Canadiana (ebook) 20190201592

ISBN 978-1-77041-583-6 (hardcover)
ISBN 978-1-77041-525-6 (softcover)
ISBN 978-1-77305-516-9 (PDF)
ISBN 978-1-77305-515-2 (EPUB)

Classification: LCC PS8637.H73 S83 2020
DDC C813'.6—DC23

The publication of *The Subtweet* has been generously supported by the Canada Council for the Arts which last year invested $153 million to bring the arts to Canadians throughout the country and is funded in part by the Government of Canada. *Nous remercions le Conseil des arts du Canada de son soutien. L'an dernier, le Conseil a investi 153 millions de dollars pour mettre de l'art dans la vie des Canadiennes et des Canadiens de tout le pays. Ce livre est financé en partie par le gouvernement du Canada.* We acknowledge the support of the Ontario Arts Council (OAC), an agency of the Government of Ontario, which last year funded 1,737 individual artists and 1,095 organizations in 223 communities across Ontario for a total of $52.1 million. We also acknowledge the contribution of the Government of Ontario through the Ontario Book Publishing Tax Credit, and through Ontario Creates for the marketing of this book.

PRINTED AND BOUND IN CANADA

PRINTING: HUME   5   4   3   2

For Whitney Houston

"Big capital uses racism, caste-ism and sexism and gender bigotry in intricate and extremely imaginative ways to reinforce itself, protect itself, to undermine democracy and to splinter resistance."

—— ARUNDHATI ROY

Neela Devaki was an original.

She was reminded of this fact shortly after she stepped out of her cab and into the Fairmont Hotel, the main site for the North by Northeast Festival. Zipping through the masses of musicians, fans and industry reps, she felt sorry for the chandeliers, which loomed above like golden flying saucers, forced to light up the dull networking that buzzed beneath them. But a conversation between two art students, draped in curated thrift wear featuring strategically placed rips and holes, brought Neela to a reluctant halt.

"I was totally working on something like this for my final project. I guess originality really is dead," one of the women sighed, taking photos of herself, duck-faced, with a pop-up art installation.

Neela skimmed the artist's statement. The frosted toothpick statues of penises were "a comment on the current global epidemic of white demasculinization." Why not just hang a red and white flag that said *Make Art Great Again*? Brevity was the true endangered species.

"You should still do it. All the good ideas are taken anyways. Isn't that kind of freeing?" replied the other.

Neela snorted. She would never offer that sort of "comfort" to a stunted peer. No wonder she was bored with most of the art she encountered.

She considered sharing with these young women that she always knew she was on the verge of invention at the precise moment when originality felt impossible. That instead of surrendering to despair, she would needle in and out and through her brain until an idea surfaced — naked, stripped of predictability and familiarity. That this process often required her to sing a phrase over and over for hours until the syllables carved their own unique melody out of hollow air. She was certain that the reiteration planted the words in her vocal chords so that when she sang them, they carried the imprint of her body. By embedding herself into her song, she muted any risk of passing off mimicry as art. Why wasn't fully committing to creation more desirable than observing what everyone else was doing and doing the same?

But defending the sanctity of originality to strangers at an art exhibit would make her seem like an egomaniac. And no one listens to a cocksure woman.

Instead, she resumed her course, shunning the other art displays jammed in between information tables, towards the elevators in the back. Once inside the ornate elevator, she furiously pushed the kissing triangles button to avoid being invaded by a friendly small-talker. When she arrived at the room for the panel, she glared at the *Race and Music* human-sized banner. Only someone who thought they didn't have a race could have come up with that title. Unable to differentiate between "panel discussions" and "group therapy sessions," she had almost declined this invitation until she beheld the glimmering word "honorarium." She wasn't in a financial position to refuse this rare offer of compensation.

A volunteer modelling last season's lilac grey hair blocked the entrance, wagging the festival brochure at Neela. "I'm sorry, but this one is full. Would you like to see the list of the other events scheduled for this afternoon?"

Neela turned away and stared at the escalator ascending into the sunlight on the main floor. Before she could rush towards it, another volunteer tapped her on the shoulder.

"Nyla! We're so glad to have you join us today."

"It's Neela. Good to be here," she lied and turned to face a man who looked like an overgrown boy or a male comedian with white-tipped, near-erupting micro volcanoes under his moustache stubble.

"Right, of course, Neela. Like 'Sheila,'" he said, playfully slapping his head. "My name is Mikey, by the way."

"Mickey?" she responded, but he didn't hear her as he placed his palm on her back and guided her into the room.

She was rarely nervous before an event and was puzzled by her uncharacteristic perspiration. She worried Mikey could feel her sweat through her ruby blouse until she realized that the wetness was coming from his hand. She shrugged casually, but his fingers clung to her, even when she stumbled over the sneakers of the men in graphic tees and chinos who had filled the standing room area at the back of the hotel ballroom.

When they reached the stage, Mikey quickly introduced her to the four panellists, three men and one woman, all of whom appeared to be in their twenties. They each greeted her with variations of "so honoured to meet you." She would have gladly reciprocated, but her diligent moderator research had left her unimpressed.

"Thank you all for joining us for today's exciting talk on race and music," Mikey announced into the mic. The audience applauded enthusiastically, their festival lanyards flapping.

"As you know . . ." He paused until the applause trailed off. "As you know, this recent issue is one that we need to think more about. And to get things started, we have . . ."

He paused again, this time interrupted by the volunteer/bouncer Neela had encountered outside the room, who was racing towards him, waving a folded note.

"Oh, and um, of course, we acknowledge we are on Indigenous land," he said. "Also, a big thank you to our sponsors. Without taking up too much more time, I want to introduce the moderator for today's panel, Nyla Devaki."

Mikey gestured at her with his sweaty hand and grinned. The audience applauded again. She smiled back at him with all of her teeth, because she was a consummate professional, even if she wasn't getting paid enough for this bullshit.

"I have her bio here, but I think it goes without saying how amazing this human is and how lucky we are to have her here with us today."

Then Mikey read the panellists' bios, each one longer than the one before, and all of them featuring copious adjectives (*visionary*, *distinct*, *powerful*, *influential*), hyperbolic comparisons to music pioneers (Billie Holiday, Marvin Gaye, Joni Mitchell), and exhaustive lists of accolades acquired from organizations that Neela had never heard of. Sedated by the monotony of manufactured praise and the stench of carpet cleaner, she almost didn't hear Mikey say, "Take it away, Nyla."

After firming her posture and taking a sip of water (that she wished was vodka), Neela posed her first question: "What do you think is your most valuable skill or trait as a racialized musician?" She'd considered starting with a softer question, perhaps one about the panellists' inspirations or current projects, but why waste time? All the male panellists reached out for her mic to respond but she handed it to the brown woman, despite her grandiose all-caps name.

"My most valuable skill as a POC singer is that I am here . . ." RUK-MINI declared, pointing to the stage. "I didn't grow up seeing musicians like me on TV or in magazines. And I still don't really see people like me out there. Representation matters, you know?"

Some people of colour in the audience poetry-snapped while the rest of the audience loudly applauded again. The slender white androgynous person who was crocheting in the first row nodded their head as vigorously as they hooked the strawberry yarn into what looked like the beginnings of a pussy hat.

Neela tousled her short-cropped hair, disturbed by the idea that simply showing up or existing was a skill. How was that different from being white? RUK-MINI beamed in her large costume gold earrings, bangles and rings; she looked like she had just stepped out from a Little India shopping spree. Maybe this is why the audience was so captivated by her, their Bollywood dreams come true.

Neela hoped that the other panellists would respond by describing their rigorous creative practices or by highlighting how they drew on their cultural ancestry or family influences. But each response was distressingly similar — a low bar and a lack of remorse (and an overuse of the word "folks"). Were they composing their answers for applause or were they being sincere? Which was worse?

"What might POC art that isn't just a response to a lack of representation or oppression sound or look like?" This was the question Neela wanted to follow up with, but she didn't think the panellists (or the audience) were interested in tackling this. Instead she asked, "Can all of you speak to the systemic barriers you face in your career and how it impacts your artistry?" still attempting to redirect the discussion to a core issue. The discussion devolved into a bitchfest about the perils of public exposure and social media. Embarrassed by the panellists' complaining, in public, about being "public personas" on Twitter, Neela kept her gaze away from the audience and on the neon-green spike tape beside her pointed flats. Given that she had never even heard of the panellists prior to this event, the real danger seemed to be that the internet made everyone believe they were a lot more famous than they actually were.

Once Neela returned home from the panel, she raced to the shower. She scrubbed her body with her loofah, hoping to wash away the memory of the panel. She couldn't brush off RUK-MINI's comment about the lack of "people like her." Presumably she meant other brown women? How could she talk about her invisibility sitting next to Neela — unless she didn't actually *see* her. Stepping out the shower, her body dripped a trail of large water coins. She beheld her reflection in the slowly defogging mirror. RUK-MINI was right. Neela was nothing like her.

Six months prior to the panel, Rukmini wouldn't have called herself a musician despite clicking away in her new basement studio space. Instead of recording, she was blowing another evening tumbling through a YouTube wormhole.

Creating her YouTube account had been a gesture of allyship. A troll had been shit-talking Too Attached in the comments for their "Diversity" video and Rukmini was livid. Her options were:

a) to continue composing clever rebuttals that would have no impact because she never posted them, or
b) to respond directly.

Popular advice was that responding was "a waste of time" and that she should "ignore the comments," but what was a better use of time than fighting hate?

She found herself procrastinating on writing her *Toronto Tops* articles about the city's Best Hot Dog Salad or Hottest Pansexual Party by visiting any of the eight boxes of "Recommended Videos" displayed at the bottom of her homepage — Kay Ray, Aparna Nancherla, Hasan Minhaj comedy clips and makeup tips. After a few weeks, she branched off into the world of daredevil stunts and gradually began paying attention to the number of views as well as the actual videos.

Before she had started her own account, YouTube had been a place to find old music videos and upcoming movie trailers. She had never thought about it as a distinct medium with its own personality. YouTube popularity seemed to defy the cultural value of aesthetics and even quality. Crisp or informative content rarely won more views. Lo-fi sibling gag videos reliably had higher stats than big-budget American music videos. This triumph of the everyday over the exceptional fascinated and comforted her. After she'd hustled through her twenties, YouTube made her feel as though she didn't have to try so hard.

Eventually, her fixation with beatboxing competition videos led her to music production lessons.

"Welcome to the twenty-first century. There are tutorials for everything on YouTube," Sumi chided when Rukmini shared her discovery before their monthly pitch meeting.

"But these videos are so comprehensive." Rukmini gestured at the YouTube page on her sticker-covered laptop. "I think there might even be a story here. Something along the lines of Toronto youth turning to YouTube for accessible education instead of traditional schools?"

"I think 'Toronto's Trending YouTubers' is closer to what they want around here, tbh."

She and Sumi had met soon after Rukmini started working at *Toronto Tops*. Rukmini had been admiring Sumi's oversized men's blazer at her first staff meeting, when Sumi said to her in a monotone, "So, you're diverse too." When Rukmini retorted, "And you must be Diverse 1?" Sumi's manicured left eyebrow had lifted.

From then on, she and Sumi always sat together at meetings and signed off emails to each other with D1 and D2. Sometimes they "accidentally" signed emails to the rest of the team with their abbreviated nicknames, which their colleagues never acknowledged. The advice columnist, a white gay guy who lived in a Front Street condo that his parents had bought for him, had once signed an email he sent them about a Pride-related pitch as D3. They didn't reply.

Sumi's dry but realistic response prevented Rukmini from making her pitch but didn't stop her from continuing to watch the tutorials. Writing for *Toronto Tops* was generally amusing and had covered her rent for the past five years, but constantly chasing a story made her feel submissive. She felt nostalgic for a time when she was more in control, when her creativity and skills were poured into something more meaningful than generating clickbait. She downloaded an illegal copy of Ableton and began relearning how to program drums.

"You should convert the basement into your office-slash-studio," her roommate Puna had suggested when Rukmini told her about her new hobby.

"Why? Am I making too much noise?" She often waited for Puna to leave the house before she did any recording.

"You don't make enough noise! This way you can be as loud as you want, no holding back."

"Okay, but what if I get murdered down there?"

"Then I definitely won't be able to hear you."

When they had moved into the house on Palmerston, they had ambitious plans to turn the cavernous basement into a screening room with a projector and folding chairs. They had even discussed programming (beginning with a Deepa Mehta retrospective), snacks (Puna's papadum mango scoops or chili lime popcorn) and charging friends and neighbours for admission to raise funds for the Toronto Rape Crisis Centre. But the dampness and darkness of the space had dissuaded them from using it as anything more than a storage dump for their suitcases and still-unpacked boxes.

Glancing up from her screen, Rukmini was impressed by how a little cleaning and a few accessories had enlivened the basement — the fairy lights she had hung along the rafters and the fuzzy rug she had relocated from the living room. But something, or someone, was missing. When she had worked upstairs, Puna's movements around the house had not only provided company, they had also offered rhythmic inspiration. Rukmini had developed a habit of using Ableton to mimic some of the muffled sounds outside her bedroom door: dishes breaking, cupboards closing and even the frenetic pace of Puna's footsteps.

Rukmini jumped from YouTube to Twitter and refreshed five times. When no new tweets appeared in her feed, she inhaled and opened Ableton. Listening to her most recent loop, an arpeggiated beat that she had built to hit progressively harder as it reached the eighth bar, it still sounded too stark. The water whirling through the pipes gave her the idea to add a tremolo effect on every other snare hit to generate a more aqueous flow, but this only enhanced the loop's hollowness. After adding two shaker sounds and tweaking the compression settings on both, she closed the file and headed upstairs, wistfully humming the song that had been in her head for weeks.

Serenading herself with Lykke Li's "Sadness Is a Blessing" had become a coping strategy to weather her annual winter depression. At the grocery store earlier that week, the song had echoed in her mind as she had sorted through the selection of pruned fruit. In frustration, she had picked up a bruised banana and whisper-sung to it, *Sadness is my boyfriend*. She closed her eyes and waited for her words to transform the produce section into a flash mob like the ones she had seen in YouTube videos, where shoppers ripped off their parkas, kicked off their boots and burst through the doors of the store to discover that their dancing had wondrously spawned summer. Instead, a man had tapped her shoulder, pulling her out of her reverie, and offered, "I could be your boyfriend?"

She paused at the top stair and turned around. At her desk, she opened her drawer, pushed aside the spare cables and pulled out the mic she had purchased to record live snaps and claps. After she set up the mic stand and adjusted it to her height, she put on the headphones Puna had gifted her and spoke into the mic. "Testing, testing" felt like posturing, so instead she talked about what she had eaten for breakfast — "Puna's lemon ricotta pancakes, maple syrup, peppermint tea." Once she saw the green levels in Ableton oscillate in response to her voice, she stopped talking and replayed the drum loop she had been working on. Then she hit record and belted *my wounded rhymes make silent cries tonight* like she had wanted to in the grocery store. Less than an hour later, she finished a rough mix.

"Is that *you?*"

"Oh my god, Puna! You scared the shit out of me! How long have you been standing there?" Rukmini quickly turned off the Lykke Li cover, regretting that she had played it through her monitors instead of listening on her headphones.

"I didn't know you could sing like that!" Puna exclaimed.

"I can't sing."

"What do you call that then?" Puna pointed at the computer, as though Rukmini's vocals had emerged from the machine. An accurate assessment.

"Filler? The drums needed something."

"Your *voice* is something. People need to hear this." Puna sat down on the green wooden chair that had been left in the basement by the previous tenant and swayed.

"You think?" Rukmini was distracted by the chair, which was squeaking in time with Puna's giddy rocking.

"Definitely! Upload it to YouTube right now!"

"Stop it. Aren't I too old to be a YouTube cover singer?" Puna had previously made fun of her late discovery of and obsession with YouTube.

"Oh, whatever. I think Susan Boyle pretty much destroyed the idea that anyone is too old to sing."

"Hey! My name is not Susan," Rukmini joked.

After Puna went back upstairs, Rukmini took a sip of her beer and opened up Photo Booth. She recorded a dimly lit video of her lip syncing her cover, rejecting the high production values of other split-screen cover videos she had seen. She made eye contact with the camera to prevent herself from looking at her reflection onscreen and laughing and didn't watch the video after she finished recording the song.

"Fuck it," she shrugged, and clicked Upload.

Neela loathed cover songs. She was an artist, not a parrot. Why would she hide behind someone else's lyrics when she could sing her own? She had also never heard a cover that sounded better than the original. Covers only made her crave the original. Was there a word for art that made her long for that which came before — besides "remake," "throwback" or "sequel"?

When "Paper Planes" had been ubiquitous in 2007, a drunk man had yelled, "Do you know any M.I.A.?" in the middle of her set at the Horseshoe Tavern.

"Someone get that jerk out of here," she had commanded.

Her words had silenced the crowd — an applause-worthy feat in any bar. Some of the audience members left, but as she picked up her song, she was pleased to have weeded out anyone who thought she should stoop so low as to sing someone else's song. They didn't deserve her.

Two weeks after North by Northeast, Neela logged into Twitter to post her daily dream recap:

> I dreamt I was a serif font running away from someone trying to cut off my serifs. It was Wes Anderson #FantasticMrFont #Futura

Then she noticed the glowing number twenty-two beside the bell icon and muttered, "Really?"

Most of her tweets didn't make it to double digit recognition. Her most popular tweet had been a photo of her eating lasagna onstage at a show at the Rivoli. The day after her birthday, her keyboard player Kasi had pulled a slice of lasagna out from behind her setup and lit the candle she had jammed into it.

After whispering, "I know you hate cake. Happy birthday, Neels," in her ear, Kasi had grabbed Neela's mic and sung "Happy Birthday," encouraging the audience to join in by waving her free hand from side to side like a conductor. Being celebrated with cold but glowing pasta had made agreeing to opening for The Turn Arounds worthwhile, even though she didn't care for their merry folk rock (how many songs with "na na na" or "oh oh oh" choruses could one band get away with?) or for their ostentatious lead singer, Marcus Young.

She clicked on the bell and scrolled through the latest tweets she had been tagged in:

Love this cover! @RUKMINI & @Neeladevaki #dreamteam

can't stop listening this song is literally #everysong #onrepeat @rukmini @neeladevaki

Apparently, the woman from the panel had covered Neela's song.

The first time Rukmini saw Neela perform live, she had been opening for The Turn Arounds at the Rivoli, a few months before North by Northeast. Tucked behind a restaurant, the venue was a generic music bar, save for the exposed brick walls: a narrow hall that smelled like prom, leading to an anti-climactic black block for a stage. Why was it never a red or fire-orange stage? Why was there never a dramatic backdrop with painted cheetahs or robots or even a floral mural? Maybe Torontonians would be more likely to check out live music if some effort was invested in creating ambience.

No one has time for that shit, Sumi had texted her as Rukmini waited in the venue for the opening acts, her ritual Sumi wanted no part of.

You're just gonna have another deadline tomorrow, D1! Just come!

LOL I bet you don't even know who the opening acts are, Sumi teased.

I don't, but who cares! What's with this city needing everyone to be vetted?

If Rukmini was going to a show, she wanted to have the beginning-to-end experience, no matter how boring the openers were likely to be, and not just to ensure a return on her investment. She found the whole concert hierarchy distressing, and if she didn't attend the entire show, she felt she was only contributing to it.

In between texts, Rukmini glanced in the direction of the door, hoping Sumi — or anyone — would show up and help fill out the sparse room. She fretted about low turnout at every show she attended, which her therapist would probably attribute to her fear of abandonment. This is why she could never perform live.

Vetting is my job *brown queen emoji*. I don't even want to see The Turn Arounds.

Neither do I. I'm doing this for you!

Very collegial of you, Sumi responded.

Rukmini took off her leather jacket, tying it around her waist. Do you think Marcus will take his shirt off? Rukmini asked, referencing his notorious abs display.

Fuck I hope not. Skinless chicken is not good for my *vegetarian lifestyle*

LOL!

Rukmini headed to the bar and ordered a beer, wishing she had brought one of Puna's quiche tarts that had been sitting on the kitchen table. But as the first few sips of beer settled inside her, her nerves and hunger settled too. She pulled her phone out of her back pocket and tweeted:

> friends don't make friends see opening acts by themselves

Would Sumi be offended? It wasn't really a subtweet. They were besties. She put her phone in her plaid shirt pocket. From her new perspective at the back of the room, a healthy crowd had gathered, though she now, thanks to Sumi, pictured everyone as skinless chickens cloaked in winter jackets.

At 9 p.m. sharp, a statuesque brown woman glided onto the stage. Rukmini gasped, recognizing her immediately. She had heard of Neela Devaki and seen photos of her online but hadn't read any commentary about her music in *Toronto Tops* or anywhere else. She seemed to be more of a local fixture, a name and a face, than a musician, which was likely why Rukmini hadn't thought to look up her work.

Neela was wearing a black dress with gold trim that tied around her neck. A train that had to be at least two metres long slithered behind her. With her emerald electric guitar in her hands, she reminded Rukmini of Versace-era Courtney Love. She shook her head, annoyed that this was one of the only references she had for a female frontwoman. The audience applauded mechanically and then resumed their chatter, but Rukmini's hands were still, clasped in prayer.

Neela stared at the crowd, silent. A minute passed, then another. The crowd began to hush and shift uncomfortably. Rukmini felt certain that Neela was clairvoyant and, like a teacher, was determining her lesson plan according to what she read in the minds of the audience members. Rukmini ducked behind a tall white man, worried that if Neela locked eyes with her, she would know that she had never given her enough attention.

When Neela finally broke her silence, Rukmini gasped again, unprepared for the bass of her vocals. Neela's voice was neither sweet nor raspy, tender nor sensual. Rukmini was reminded of her grandfather's death, and the two weeks her family had spent beside his hospital bed, waiting for him to pass. His room had smelled sour, despite the growing number of bouquets of not-quite-white-but-not-quite-pink carnations fighting with the boxes of Timbits for table space. Listening to the sound of his laboured breathing and coughing fits made her wish she too would escape her own body. When she later described Neela's voice to Puna, she said that it sounded like the feeling of watching someone die, like witnessing every leaf on a deciduous tree change colour and fall as autumn transitioned into winter.

Rukmini wept for the duration of Neela's thirty-minute set that seemed to render the entire stage aglow. Tall Man turned around mid-show and offered her his checkered handkerchief. Given her state, she wasn't able to refuse it, despite its revolting aftershave scent.

As Neela strode offstage, Rukmini rushed out of the bar, still clutching the soggy handkerchief. She forgot about The Turn Arounds. She forgot about Sumi. She drifted through Chinatown, kicking the fresh snow and humming the melody of Neela's closing number.

Every song's about falling in love or breaking up
Nobody's singing to me

When Neela learned from her Twitter feed that RUK-MINI had covered her song, she rolled her eyes and ignored the cover. Until she saw she was tagged in a write-up by *Sheep & Goat*.

> Underground Canadian jazz singer @NeelaDevaki's Every Song reshaped into breathtaking classic by cover singer @RUKMINI

Her spine straightened. Although she rarely agreed with their reviews, even a mention on this music blog could boost a musician's career. She wasn't sure if she was more vexed that she was finally being featured because of a cover or that the blog covered covers. She also wished the word "jazz" came with a trigger warning. While her music featured the occasional horn or upright bass, and she did revel in Ella and Nina on rained-in weekends, decoded, "jazz" always read to her as "we aren't sure how to describe your music because it doesn't sound white."

And the word "breathtaking." When she had released her debut album eight years ago, she had almost forgotten to put on her shoes before she hastened to the indigo *Toronto Tops* box by her bus stop, straps still unbuckled. She opened the rusted box and breathed in the smell of freshly inked words. After grabbing the third copy from the top, to avoid the ones that had already been flipped through, she knelt and spread the paper out on the sidewalk. When she reached the new releases page, she scanned for her name above the paragraph-long reviews. She almost didn't see it in the bottom right corner.

Neela Devaki (self-titled) 3.5/5
An interesting combination of sounds shows Neela Devaki is not just a pretty face (as featured on her breathtaking album cover), but a musician to watch.

As she reread the review, she noticed that her fingernails were digging into her cheek. She hadn't spent four years painstakingly writing songs and saving up to record them to be *watched*. She then scratched her nails into the paper until there was a hole where her review had been. When she finally stood up, she chucked the paper in the recycling bin on the other side of the bus stop.

Since then, equally vague and inappropriate comments about her appearance coupled with occasionally polite comments about her music had been published, but she dreamed of being known for writing a classic, timeless song. Reading the *Sheep & Goat* headline, she reminded herself that some musicians — or rather wannabe musicians like cover singers (who were basically karaoke singers) — were more attached to being *timely* and an immediate sense of connection. But she wanted everlasting. She wanted to write songs that burrowed so innocuously into a listener's psyche until the melody became not familiar, but family. Blood.

As her eyes skimmed over the article, she shuddered at the words "electro treatment." If anything, she had intended for "Every Song" to have a country sound and still regretted not searching for a pedal steel guitarist because she had assumed she wouldn't be able to find a female musician. Imagining her lyrics washed over with predictable synths, she refused to click Play. When would musicians get tired of referencing the eighties? What had happened from 2000 onward to instill an insecurity so insurmountable that it halted the exploration of new sounds? Why had nostalgia become a genre in and of itself?

Neela had laboured to create a body of work that was singular. When listeners heard a Neela Devaki album, they would think, *This sounds like nothing I have heard before*. She recalled lying on the discoloured carpet of the basement apartment she had been sharing in Kensington, gripping her electric guitar with pride when she had finished composing "Every Song." She knew she had just written one of her best songs.

I got your hair caught in my teeth again
I don't want to spit it out

The reviews she imagined would declare:

These opening lines are Devaki's finest lyrics yet, not just because of their physicality and sensuality, but because of their repulsiveness.

This is the closest Neela Devaki has come to expressing love in a song, that feeling of urgent and ugly desire.

But there was a price to pay for being distinct in a field named *popular*. She understood that her job was to write songs that hooked, that transformed listeners into addicts, and she defied her duties at her own peril. So when no such insightful reviews were ever written, she managed her disappointment in her usual manner: she wrote another song.

Now, eight years later, journalists were finally emailing her questions about "Every Song" — RUK-MINI's cover of it.

What did you think when you heard the track?

How do you feel about the enormous response the cover has received?

She wasn't sure how to answer these questions diplomatically and deleted the messages. The song was *hers*, and these reporters had the audacity to ask her to comment on a rendering. Would a painter be expected to comment enthusiastically on a forgery? She opened a blank Word document and compiled a list of questions she would prefer to be asked:

> What part of "Every Song" did you write first — the verses, the chorus or the bridge?
>
> How did you get your guitar tone?
>
> Why was the song never released as a single?

She wished she could as easily delete the pressure that she felt to retweet RUK-MINI's cover, or one of the many music blog posts that had preceded this *Sheep & Goat* review. As her mouse hovered over the retweet symbol, she was pained by how similar it was to the recycle symbol. She wondered if "Every Song" had been better off being mostly undiscovered, discarded in the vast landfill of songs that were never heard, instead of being mined for its parts. She wanted a way to click on just half of the button, the part with the arrow going down, to somehow suppress the circulation of the cover. A detweet.

Instead, she grudgingly typed RUK-MINI in the Twitter search box. **34K** followers. She swallowed and opened her own profile in a new tab. **2,487** followers. She examined her recent tweets — had she been using the platform wrong?

> What is the word for the feeling of dipping your feet in a body of water?

Was the standardization of pitch to A440 just another form of white supremacy?

Hot date with Martin Goodman trail tomorrow morning.

Had she not tweeted enough memes or travel photos? Was her grammar too precise? Did she not use caps lock enough? She composed a tweet — u suck lol stop trying to be me LMAO — smirked, then deleted it.

She looked out her window, admiring the patches of white daisies shooting out around the edges of the front lawn. She had always wanted to live on a street where the trees on either side of the road reached for each other and touched in the middle, creating a bridge of leaves and branches that she sometimes imagined crossing from her top-floor apartment like a high-wire artist. She also appreciated that her banana-coloured house stood out on the street like a mistake that no one had bothered to correct.

Now calmer, she flipped back to RUK-MINI's Twitter page. Her bio read, covers culture and songs but never my eyes. In her profile photo, her eyelids were kohl-smudged and her left eyebrow was cocked. Then Neela noted the light-grey declaration: Follows you.

Below this, the pinned tweet:

was so inspired after meeting my fave @neeladevaki last week. had to cover "every song." this song is every thing xoxo

How had Neela not seen this tweet before? Her throat relaxed and so did her fingers on her mouse. She clicked the retweet symbol to prove she could be equally generous.

Then the cursor continued to move on its own and clicked Follow.

Neela hoped that Rukmini would cancel.

As she travelled west on the lethargic Queen streetcar, Neela repeatedly checked Twitter, awaiting a last-minute message. She intermittently checked the time on her phone and eventually tweeted:

> "Apathy": the Queen streetcar's relationship to your schedule.

When she had clicked on the envelope icon at the top of her Twitter page the week before, she was surprised to discover Rukmini had sent her a direct message and suggested meeting up. Then she remembered that asking someone out for coffee in this city was the equivalent to asking, "How are you?" in passing, never waiting for the response. No one was actually interested in sitting across from a relative stranger, squirming through the awkward process of getting to know a new adult. She had replied plainly, "We should," assuming Rukmini wouldn't respond, but she promptly did with several dates and times when she was available, closing her message with

Rukmini's use of the unstylized version of her name puzzled Neela. It seemed informal, like they were already friends. But she was more disturbed by Rukmini's use of "love," her ability to grant this word, saturated with monumental meaning, to a stranger.

Regretting her decision to meet Rukmini and irritated by the irreverence of twenty-somethings, she considered not showing up. She pictured Rukmini waiting for her at Grapefruit Moon, the café on Bathurst she had suggested. Rukmini would look at her phone, avoiding her server's pitying look and refreshing her inbox, checking for a message that would not arrive. At first, Rukmini would worry, wondering if something dreadful had happened to Neela. Eventually Rukmini's paranoia would turn on her, and she would fret that she had somehow been offensive or too forward, that maybe she should have used the word "dear" as a greeting rather than "hey" and definitely should not have signed off with "love."

When Neela arrived at Grapefruit Moon on time, she felt claustrophobic from its congested layout of rustic tables crammed together. If she left immediately, Rukmini would never know she had been there. As she backed towards the door, she heard, "Fuck!" She had stepped on someone.

"I'm sorry." She turned.

"Neela! Hi!"

"Rukmini?" With her hair in a loose bun and no jewellery, she didn't look the way Neela remembered her from North by Northeast.

"Ya!"

"Your foot . . . is it . . ."

"Oh, it's fine. Honestly. You can step on me anytime!" Rukmini laughed, hugging her, and added, "I love your skirt." Neela had paired the pencil skirt with a pinstriped blouse, like she was on a hiring committee. She felt perturbed by Rukmini's nonchalant outfit: a cut-up crop top and jeans.

"Sit anywhere," called the dishevelled server from behind the bar counter.

Rukmini threw her worn canvas purse on the table by the front window. There was a loose thread hanging from the trunk of the pink elephant embroidered on the top flap of her bag. Was she a cross-stitcher? "Aah," Rukmini sighed.

"Are you in pain?" Neela craned her neck to look under the table.

"No, no. It's so great to finally hang out, Neela. One-on-one, you know?" She pronounced Neela the Indian way, emphasizing the *n* and *l*.

"It is," she said, envying the cyclist who had just rode by — free, outside.

"So. Can I ask you something?"

Neela never knew how to respond to this question,

which always suggested a more invasive question was on its way. She nodded slightly.

"What did you think?"

Was Rukmini asking her thoughts on the North by Northeast panel? How would Neela respond politely?

"You two ready?" the server interjected, pen hovering above a notepad.

"I'll have the peppermint tea with agave," Rukmini stated, like a regular. How many friend dates had Rukmini brought there? Did she always sit in the same spot? Had they all met online?

"I guess I'll have the same." More of a ginger tea woman, Neela didn't like peppermint but felt an unfamiliar impulse to seem agreeable.

"My cover!" Rukmini continued as though they hadn't been interrupted.

"Oh." It hadn't occurred to her that Rukmini would want to discuss the cover. Was this why she had asked to meet? Wasn't it enough that Neela had retweeted her?

"Oh no. You hate it!" Rukmini covered her mouth with her ombre manicured fingers.

"No, I liked it."

"Oh good! I'm so relieved. Ever since I saw you perform it at the Rivoli in March, it's been in my head."

"You were there?" She found it easier to picture Rukmini at a mega pop concert at the Rogers Centre than at one of her own shows. Rukmini seemed like the kind of woman who would be on her feet for the whole concert, dancing and screaming with her girlfriends, forcing the people sitting behind them to stand.

"Two peppermint teas?" the server announced, placing large baby blue mugs in front of them. He paused. "By the way, you're Neela Devaki, right?" he whispered.

She nodded.

"I'm a big fan."

"You should see her live if you haven't already!" Rukmini shouted as he raced back to the kitchen before Neela could even say thank you.

"Seriously though, what a show," Rukmini continued, clasping her cheeks with her hands in awe. "I love how you grabbed the audience's attention with *silence* of all things. Kind of genius. And your voice, my god. I cried the whole time."

"Really?" Neela tilted her head.

"Embarrassing, but I couldn't help it. And then when your keyboard player brought out the lasagna? So sweet!"

"Kasi. She really made it a special night."

"Hmm," she crooned and nodded.

Softened by Rukmini's un-Toronto-like generosity and enthusiasm (or by the agave in the tea), Neela blurted, "Actually, I agreed to meet you because I loved your cover."

"You did?" Rukmini pumped her fist, as though the Leafs had just scored.

Neela had been so certain she would hate the cover that the first time she listened to it, she had pressed Play on the YouTube link and retreated to the washroom, leaving the door barely open. When the song opened with the expected fuzzy synth line, Neela sarcastically muttered, "Breathtaking." But as the song continued, she became mesmerized by Rukmini's bright harmonies that she had found to complement the lead. From the toilet, she reached out to pull the door open. Unlike a lot of the electronic music she disliked, the drums didn't drown out the track but instead intensified the devotion expressed in her lyrics. Without flushing, she strode back to her computer, opened iTunes and played her original song to confirm its superior status. Midway into the chorus, she unconsciously began singing Rukmini's harmonies. Later when she sank into her bed like a wounded warrior grateful for sunset, Rukmini's cover continued playing in her head. Since that night, she had been unable to sleep.

"You took something I thought was already pretty perfect and made it more so. That's power."

"Power. Interesting word choice."

Embarrassed that she had offered too much praise, she thought about also confessing that she had hoped meeting Rukmini would somehow restore her own power, that maybe, like in a myth, when Rukmini's mouth opened, Neela's song would escape and return to her, its rightful owner. Instead she asked, "Have you ever thought about recording your own material?"

Rukmini bowed her head over her empty mug. "No.

Covers are my thing, I guess." She used air quotes to emphasize *thing*.

Feeling guilty, Neela thought about asking the server for more hot water. "They don't have to be?" she offered.

"Hmm." Rukmini paused. "You and I should start a band!" she announced, sitting up taller.

"A cover band?"

Rukmini let out an incredulous *ha*. "You don't do covers."

"How do you know that?" As she reached for her phone to check the time, Rukmini put her hand on Neela's.

"Neela Devaki, I know everything about you."

"How did it go?" Puna yelled from the kitchen when Rukmini got home.

Whenever she tried to guess what Puna was making based on the smells that seeped into her bedroom, she consistently failed. What smelled like an omelette to her turned out to be crème brûlée, oatmeal turned out to be blueberry pie. But she kept guessing because she liked the adventure of testing herself and being corrected, the reminder that even her senses — her life guides — could be improved upon, strengthened.

"I don't know. Is that roasted yams?" Rukmini deflected, hanging up the jacket Puna had left on the couch in the front closet. She tolerated Puna's untidiness because of her inventive culinary skills — which she employed as head chef at the trendy and conveniently close tapas bar Bar Raval — and her magnanimous leftovers.

"Fried plantains! But tell me about Neela," Puna pressed, without leaving her domain.

"She was different from how she was at the panel. More tentative."

"Like, cold?"

"No, like . . . afraid. I told her that I would like to be friends and you should have seen her face," Rukmini walked into the kitchen and played *Freeze!*, imitating Neela's blank expression.

"Aww." Puna wiped her hands on her yellow chef coat, a tall daffodil in the wild kitchen. She kissed Rukmini's cheek. "They're almost ready, okay? Gimme ten." Puna turned her attention back to the stove. "First hangouts are always awkward."

"True." Rukmini tried to ignore the cutting board sloped against the backsplash, dripping sticky juice onto the counter. Puna was used to having others clean up for her, but Rukmini would tackle the mess later, once her stomach was warm with sautéed sweetness.

Puna shook the pan, the plantains crackling. "Or maybe she really is afraid of you!"

"She should be! I'm a nightmare!"

She expected Puna to laugh, but she didn't. Or maybe she did and Rukmini didn't hear her as she ambled to her bedroom. After she landed on her bed, she flipped through the selfies that she and Neela had taken before they had left the café, swinging her calves and feet in the air.

"Do you like this one?" She had handed Neela her phone after selecting the photo she thought was most flattering to Neela, emphasizing her chiselled cheek-bones. Neela had looked anywhere but at the camera in every shot. She assumed this was because Neela, like most people, didn't like how she looked in photos. But Neela wasn't like most people. If Neela's discomfort wasn't so obvious, Rukmini would have added, "God, you're beautiful."

"Any of them are fine." Neela pushed open the café door, letting the wind smack around the *Open* sign, without turning back to look at the phone.

"Do you have a favourite filter?"

"Do you?" Remembering Neela's crisp tone here, it occurred to her that maybe Neela didn't want to be in a photo with *her*. Maybe Puna was right.

"I generally hashtag no filter because they seem to only make me look lighter than I am, and I'm already seen as not brown enough."

"Yeah, photography is optimized for white skin." Neela rolled up her sleeves, as if to offer her dark sepia skin to the sun in defiance.

"Really? I guess everything is, but I'm still always surprised."

She posted their photo on Instagram, sans filter, tagging Neela, with the caption:

hung out with this legend today!!!!

She clicked on Neela's handle and scanned her photos. Neela was in very few of them. Her grid was all plants, park settings and skyline sunsets, symmetrically composed. Rukmini then searched under Following. Neela followed ALOK, Heleena Tattoos, Nimisha Bhanot and other South Asian creatives — but not her. Why hadn't Neela followed her back? Were these artists more skilled? Was their brownness more apparent because of how clearly it was a part of their work? Were their numbers more impressive? Or had Neela just not yet seen Rukmini's account?

Flipping back to her own account, she reviewed her grid of mostly selfies, alone or with her friends, and photos of Puna's cooking, trying to imagine what Neela would think. Basic? She chewed on the hangnail on her thumb. Had she blown it with Neela, making a poor first impression in real life and online?

She bounced back to Neela's profile and clicked on Message beneath her profile photo (a pointy succulent planted in a cream conch) to send her a damage control DM:

so great to meet with you today! excited about our band xoxo

Then she tucked her phone under her pillow, grabbed the basket of dirty laundry in her closet and trekked to the basement. With every item she tossed into the washer's gaping mouth, she dissected every sentence she could recall saying to Neela, analyzing the implications of her words and how they might have been misinterpreted.

Had she raved too much about Neela's show or song, like the excess teal detergent drooling off the rim of its bottle in her grip? Had she come across like a starry-eyed fan? Had she embarrassed Neela? Or herself? She'd read interviews where celebrities talked about never knowing who to trust, who their real friends were. Did Neela think she wanted something from her? She regretted suggesting they form a band, even though she was sure it was a brilliant idea.

As she returned to her room, she mentally art-directed the photoshoot for their first album cover. Against a tiger orange background, their bodies, wrapped in brown fabric, would be entangled in a way to convey both tenderness and an impermeable bond. Sisters.

She interpreted the eighty-seven notifications on her phone — all likes and comments on their selfie — as confirmation that their band would be a success. As the likes continued to climb, she revisited her own selfies from the previous week to compare the numbers. None of them had as many likes as the new one with Neela. She tried to tell herself that the popularity of their photo was because it featured *both* of them — double the interest, double the likes. But as evening plunged into night, she became more certain that the likes were strictly for Neela.

Before she fell asleep, her thumb wavered over the photo.

Then she clicked Delete.

Neela didn't expect to see Rukmini again.

When a first coffee date did happen in the city, it was rarely followed by a second. Instead, the coffee date functioned as urban social taste-testing. There was always a fresh, edgy artist emerging from the concrete every few months. Meeting with them was not only a way of raising one's own profile, it was also restorative to discover that "new" artists weren't actually as interesting or as talented as everyone had proclaimed — or as poised as they appeared on social media. After they would finish touting the umpteen projects they were toiling on — making video art about their pregnant hamster and writing a poetry book entitled *Sufferin Street* and launching a shareable underwear line for gay couples — their stamina and sheen would predicatably fade. Nothing destroyed mystery like hearing a supposedly groundbreaking artist confess familiar insecurities, or watching them chew on a ham sandwich and deciding when to mention the bit of kale wedged in their front teeth. Neela herself had been sampled and spat out many times, and although she knew that this behaviour "wasn't personal" and that people were "very busy," she restricted the number of coffee date requests she obliged and quit drinking coffee altogether.

She assumed Rukmini had gotten what she wanted out of their coffee date — a selfie, proof of their association (though surprisingly Rukmini never posted it). A few days later, when Neela clicked on the paper airplane icon in the top right-hand corner of her Instagram account, she found two DMs from Rukmini:

> so great to meet with you today! excited about our band xoxo

> Hey Neela! When are we hanging out again? 416-852-1472

Neela stood up from her desk and bent her knee into a warrior pose while looking at her phone. After a minute, she sat back down and gave in.

Hi Rukmini. Neela here. I'm free on Saturday.

Rukmini texted back instantly. Neela! How about Friday? Shani Mootoo is speaking at Harbourfront. She included a link with more information about the event.

Oh, I would have loved that. Cereus Blooms is one of my favourite books. Unfortunately, I have a big Canada Council grant deadline to meet.

Neela glanced up from her phone to the budget spreadsheet cage on her computer and contemplated the freedom she'd gain by adding several zeros to the numbers she had entered in every cell for her living and recording expenses, and clicking Submit.

Same! I read it in my postcolonial lit class in undergrad. First time I encountered a self-assured brown trans character in a book. A rare combo!

His name was Otoh right? He is definitely memorable. That book is art.

Stepping away from her computer again, Neela walked to her alphabetically organized bookshelf to locate her copy of Shani's book, phone in hand.

Aren't all books technically works of art?

Only if the writing is noteworthy.

She set *Cereus* on her bedside table to reread, Rukmini's messages reminding her of the pile of books in her bedroom closet she intended to dispose of at the library.

Ha ha! So you don't think writers are inherently artists?

No. Anyone can write a book these days, Neela texted and then put her phone down on her bed and stacked the books from her closet beside the front door so she wouldn't forget to get rid of them at last. The weight of the books grew heavier as she thought about their contents — what little she could remember of them. How could so many words, so many sentences, amount to so little impact?

When she picked up her phone again, Rukmini had texted back. True. One of my fave tweets is by @rawiya: "listen it's ok to not write a book."

Exactly.

Well, I'm so curious to find out what other books you like. I want to read them :) Good luck with your grant app! *Stressed face emoji* Why don't you just come over on Saturday? We can chill!

Chill. What did that involve? That Saturday, she walked slowly to Rukmini's house, inviting the muscular humidity, her summer companion, to encase her body. She tried to recall the last time she had made a friend. In grade school, her classmates always unravelled to be less interesting than she had imagined they were in her head. She eventually traded being allured by someone's potential (and feeling the disappointment that ensued) for her own company. This had been the appeal of Twitter — a forum to engage with herself as often and as freely as she wanted and, even better, to document her thoughts. Often, when she began to write a song, she would pull up her Twitter page and pluck from her recent tweets as a lush garden of ideas.

In her twenties, most of her social interactions had felt like she was trapped in a teen drama house party but without the drama (or the teens), repeating the same small talk and catch-ups until her mouth was dried out and blistered. Occasionally these interactions would mature into friendship, but after discussing zodiac signs, favourite TV shows and movies and sharing family and relationship histories, all that was left to talk about was the latest co-worker or roommate fiasco that had collected since last seeing each other. The words "friend" and "dumpster" inevitably became synonymous.

When she approached a row of army-green compost bins on the sidewalk, she paused and reconsidered her visit to Rukmini's place. What if they ran out of stimulating topics to discuss? How much did they actually have in common? What if Rukmini just wanted to take more selfies together? Neela shuddered and grabbed her phone from her pocket to check the time — was it too late to cancel?

Rukmini had texted her. See you soon!

Persuaded by Rukmini's excitement, Neela wiped the sweat off her forehead with her arm and continued walking while checking her other notifications.

Kasi had also texted her. Rehearsal at 9 tomorrow? Will grab you a tea on the way.

Her relationship with Kasi blurred the line between friend and colleague. Three years ago, Neela had been flipping through *Toronto Tops* when she had spotted Kasi in a photo with The Turn Arounds, who were then going by MY Turn Arounds. (Kasi later revealed that "MY" was supposed to be a clever reference to Marcus Young's initials, but no one ever caught it.) Surrounded by three shirtless white men with beards, Kasi commanded the stage in her white tank top and zippered punk pants. Even though she was positioned to the side, she looked like the lead singer, her blue-black shag wailing with sweat. When Neela read the article, it mentioned Kasi only once, identifying her as the keyboardist. At the time, Neela had been brainstorming ways to elevate her live show and as soon as she saw that photo, she was certain that including

Kasi was the answer. Never one to be seduced by mere presentation, Neela had emailed Kasi an invitation to her rehearsal space so that she could decide if Kasi had the necessary chops.

"Thanks for agreeing to meet with me." Neela had reached her hand out. When she shook Kasi's, Neela appreciated their immediate equilibrium — neither one squeezed harder than the other.

"It was actually perfect timing. The MY Turn Arounds schedule is a little up in the air as they sort out their next album, so I'm looking for other work. Can I ask how you heard of me?"

"I saw a photo in *Toronto Tops*."

"Ugh. That photo." Kasi had been removing her hoodie and briefly remained under the black fleece. "I think they're using it as their official press shot."

"I thought it was just a live photo?" Neela looked away at the wall, plastered with old gig posters, to give Kasi privacy. She had always maintained that awkwardness was a feeling or behaviour largely invented by attention-seekers (the same kind who loved to share how "nerdy" their tastes were) but now felt unsettled by not knowing how to behave in the presence of another woman in a music space.

"It is, but people have been really responding to it."

"You mean people have been responding to *you*."

"Pretty much. I think they're still sorting out their brand and what's better than a Spice Girl in the mix? Can

I set up over there?" Kasi pointed to the corner of the room with the fewest stacked gear cases.

"Sure. Let me know if you need any help," Neela offered while she fidgeted with a tambourine, rattling it. "So you aren't an official member of the band?"

"Nope. And I don't really want to be. Right now they pay me as a tour musician, which is more than I would make if I was in the band. But there are other costs that come with my involvement with them. Shit." Kasi bit her thumb after she hit the button on the power bar.

"Shit," Neela echoed and stepped towards her. "Did you get electrocuted?"

"No, I'm just sorry to go on and on. It's not very professional complaining about one gig while auditioning for another, is it?"

"But I asked. I was curious about your dynamics when I saw that photo."

"What's that saying about photos and a thousand words?" Kasi's silver-ring-adorned fingers hopped on a few chords. "Anyways, I'm ready. What should I play for you?"

"Whatever you want. Whatever you think best showcases your skills." Neela sat down on a drum stool to calm her displaced nerves and felt relieved that the drummer who rented the space next door wasn't impressing himself with his erratic drum fills at that moment.

"How about something from your first album?" Kasi tinkled the first notes of "Every Song" before Neela could respond. It turned out that she had not only listened to

Neela's album several times in preparation for their meeting but had also taught herself the keyboard parts from three of the songs. Neela was mesmerized by Kasi's astrology-inspired tattoos, which seemed to shimmer as she played, her arms the colour of a dusk horizon. Before they parted ways, Neela invited Kasi to play with her at her next gig later in the month.

Since then, their relationship had grown, a product of time repeatedly spent in the company of another. Not like a rose, with delicate petals and sharp thorns, but like a backyard tree — steady, reliable. She knew that in an emergency, Kasi would be there for her, but they seldom spent time together outside of rehearsals or shows.

Now outside Rukmini's oval-glass door, Neela noted that her connection to Rukmini was also technically career-related, but somehow she orbited closer to friendship. Was this because she still didn't think of Rukmini as a musician or a peer?

Or maybe Rukmini was just an anomaly.

Since her first visit, Neela never came over empty-handed. She often brought daisies from her yard, and last week, Neela had given Rukmini a Meera Sethi *Upping the Aunty* postcard.

"This is beautiful!" Rukmini glided her fingers over the protective plastic cover. "She actually looks a little like my aunty." Leading the way to her bedroom, Rukmini asked, "What do you think of the South-Asian-artists-depicting-aunties trend?"

"Mostly, I think it's lovely. Honouring brown women who are often cast aside."

"Mostly?" Rukmini chided. Her favourite Neela thoughts were the ones she held back. Rukmini leaned on the door frame, surveying her room for the perfect spot to display the postcard. Maybe next to the thumb-tacked Janelle Monáe ticket.

"Well, sometimes I wonder who made the first aunty homage art piece and how many artists are now ripping off that artist." Neela typed on her phone and then passed it to Rukmini. "See?"

Rukmini studied the cubist painting of an older brown woman on a different artist's Instagram account. "Hmm. Are they ripping off or expanding the aunty love? This person's style is so different from Meera's. Ooh, side note! Should we listen to Rihanna's *Anti*?"

These afternoons in her bedroom reminded Rukmini of teenage friendship. They sat in her room for hours listening to her vinyl collection, often with their legs like ladders against the wall and pillows tucked under their backs, talking about production aesthetics, liner notes and their alternate choices for an album's first single. Whenever Rukmini played electronic music, Neela became silent and zoned out on her phone — unless it was Björk.

"OK. Fuck, marry, kill Björk albums. Go!" Rukmini

47

demanded the week after they had listened to Björk's discography from beginning to end.

"One second." After Neela arranged all of the Björk albums chronologically on the floor, she kneeled over them and declared, "Well, I would marry *Vespertine*, for sure."

"Oooh, what a silent and solid marriage."

"I would kill *Volta*," Neela said, lightly tossing the album on the bed where Rukmini was nestled.

"But the Timbaland songs!" Rukmini sat up and shook *Volta* in the air, like a protest poster.

"I know. But one album has to die."

"Fuck *Post*?" they said in unison and nodded sensually at each other.

Neela examined the Orange Crush–coloured backside of the *Post* vinyl jacket. "Can you believe it was made over two decades ago?"

"I was in grade six, I think. Or grade five?" Rukmini remembered refusing to get her own teeth checked for years after flipping to MuchMusic and catching a few seconds of the creepy video with the gorilla dentist.

"Really? Me too."

"1985?"

"1985?" Neela repeated as a question, her voice slightly raised. "I assumed I was older than you."

"You mean, you assumed *I* was younger than *you*."

Rukmini stood up from her bed and collected all the albums off the floor. As she slid them back on the bookshelf, she could feel Neela's eyes on her. Did she think Rukmini was immature? And if that was the case, why did Neela keep hanging out with her? Not wanting to follow these questions to answers she might not like, she turned around and did her best Björk impression. "Eets all zo quieth . . ."

This seemed to swing Neela out of her own thought vacuum, and she laugh-whispered, "Shh! Shh!"

Going back and forth, they continued singing the opening verse of "It's All So Quiet," melodramatically acting out the lines with awestruck eyes and scolding index fingers, belting out the chorus in unison. She loved hearing their voices twist together, even in jest. She especially loved watching Neela sing, the way her voice didn't seem to come from her mouth but every part of her. Even her nose seemed to vibrate when she sang.

After their singing tapered off, Rukmini threw her arms around Neela and confessed, "I really like you."

Neela had developed an internal dialogue with Rukmini.

The Rukmini in her mind was always asking questions. As Neela cycled through her morning sun salutations in her apartment, back flat and head hanging, her inner Rukmini asked, "You know how you can remember all the words to a song you haven't heard in years? Where do you think all of those songs are stored in the body?"

Before she had realized that Rukmini had invaded her mind, these questions and the process of pursuing an answer — dreaming a thought she had never thought before — had been intoxicating. She pictured every song she had ever loved (or hated) condensed into whole notes that occupied the soles of her feet.

"Why your feet?" Rukmini asked.

"Because music is the foundation."

"Hmm," the Rukmini in her mind responded and then would offer how she thought songs were sealed in her elbows or another peculiar place. When they had first started spending time together, Rukmini's incessant *hmm*s had irritated Neela. Their wordlessness, their vagueness, had suggested condescension. But in time, she had begun to appreciate each *hmm* and to respect Rukmini for having the maturity to know when formal language was necessary and when sound, on its own, was enough.

Lately though, she had become concerned that the constant presence of Rukmini's voice in her thoughts was a sign that they were spending too much time together. Neela's other internal voices were unsure about this intrusion. *Be wary of codependency*, they said. This warning was easy to shrug off. She had been in codependent relationships before, and while it was wise to maintain boundaries, to avoid the melding of two humans into a formless blob, she felt quite intact. If anything, she felt motivated by Rukmini's self-possession and had been doing yoga more frequently, to push and flex herself more regularly. But when another internal voice commented, *She probably doesn't have a Neela in her head*, she had no response.

Last week, she had lined up an hour before the doors opened for the Swet Shop Boys show because Rukmini wanted to be close to the stage. Frustrated that Rukmini was late, Neela had mentally compiled a list of tasks that she could have been attending to at home, as though fixating on them would somehow complete them.

"This venue is a strange choice for these guys," Rukmini observed in her ear after she finally arrived, embracing her and offering no apology for her tardiness.

One of the qualities she liked most about Rukmini, besides her bewitching ability to transform her appearance on a daily basis (that night Rukmini's hair was pulled back in a boundless ponytail and her baby hairs were slicked down) was that she wasn't hesitant about starting a conversation — and never resorted to the obligatory "hello," a Canadian complaint about the weather or even a recap about her day at the office. She knew that Rukmini was a journalist. She knew that before she had started working at *Toronto Tops*, she had freelanced under the pen name Ben Travers because it meant she earned more money, more respect from peers and less online vitriol.

Rukmini still associated her work life with her alter-ego Ben, occasionally mentioning that "Ben is writing about the wheatgrass popsicle craze," or "maybe Ben should investigate why that storefront has been boarded up for two years." How ingenious Rukmini was to give her day job persona a separate name. Neela wished everyone would do the same, thereby protecting their real selves and their precious non-office time. Sometimes she would ask politely, "How is Ben today?" but Rukmini seldom wanted to talk about him. Neela was grateful, not because she was disinterested but because her own work life wasn't worth nattering about either.

When she wasn't researching and applying for arts grants, she typed away her days transcribing interviews for photography magazines that hired her through a temp agency. The handful of photography night courses she had taken years ago at the Toronto City College turned out to be good for something.

"A refurbished movie theatre *is* a bit of an unusual setting, but there are fewer options for shows in this city than there used to be," Neela replied, pulling up their tickets on her phone.

"I swear there was a metal show here last week. At the Danforth Music Hall! By the way, I love your bracelet."

Had she gone to that show? She pictured Rukmini head-banging in her worn-out leather jacket and was both relieved and disappointed that she hadn't been invited. "Do you just compliment people to get them to like you?"

"What? No, I actually like your bracelet," Rukmini said and reached out for Neela's wrist to examine it closer. "I saw something like that on Queen, but in silver, and I still regret not buying it."

"Oh. Thank you. I was joking," she added, embarrassed that her mental filter had failed to hide her suspicion of sincerity, like a stereotypical Torontonian.

"Do you think that Heems ever feels jealous about Riz being the star?" Rukmini deftly changed the subject once they were inside and in line at the bar, pointing at the DIY shirt she had screen-printed with a photo of the boys performing at Coachella.

"I'm not sure Heems sees it that way."

"I just think it would be hard to be in a band with someone who was in *Star Wars*."

At first, she had found Rukmini's endless opinions and curiosity overbearing, in part because she had assumed these qualities were exclusive to people in their twenties. But Rukmini had managed to preserve these qualities into her thirties. Rukmini made her reflect on how much she missed not always feeling right or sure, how uncertainty was a gift that could lead to adventure or an opportunity to discover something new. Like when Rukmini suggested they try eating at the restaurant without lights or riding the Zipper at the Ex — both of which Neela thought she would hate and actually, astonishingly, enjoyed.

"Didn't expect to see a piano onstage," Rukmini noted, after they secured their spot, standing two rows of people away from the stage.

"Me neither. Opening act?" Neela tried not to observe the stage too closely to supress the ache she often felt when she went to shows, wishing she was on it.

"There isn't one, I checked. Do you play?"

"Piano? Never live. That's Kasi's domain. It's more of a writing tool for me." She also avoided the piano's gaze to supress the ache she felt from being unable to write songs lately.

"Hmm."

"Sometimes I challenge myself to compose with other instruments, but the piano is always the origin. Home." The ache stirred. She clasped her chest.

"That's an interesting word choice," Rukmini said.

"Which?"

"Home. I can totally imagine you living inside a piano."

Rukmini turned her back to the stage and stretched her phone out in front of her.

"Would you come visit?" Neela asked and also shifted around, recognizing the selfie-time cue. Rukmini propped her head on Neela's shoulder and adjusted her arm until the piano was visible behind them.

"Obviously!"

She tried to imagine herself opening a piano lid and crawling in to sleep every night. Others tended to see her solitude as a deficiency, exemplified by the inevitable question, "Are you seeing anyone?" But Rukmini's ability to envision her living in a piano made Neela feel as though she saw the richness in her reclusiveness and her partnership with music.

"What would you do if Kasi came out and was their piano player tonight?"

"That would be the best surprise ever."

"Right? She'd destroy that thing," Rukmini said and chugged her beer.

"I always forget that you saw her at my show. I should introduce you two. You would like each other." Neela added this to her internal task list.

"I'd love that. Hey, how about Home Keys?" Rukmini suggested, jingling imaginary house keys with her hand.

At some point in every conversation, and always at Rukmini's instigation, they would resume brainstorming names for their hypothetical band. She had wondered if Rukmini was joking about the band when they first met, but she brought it up every time they were together. Sometimes this name game would last an hour, and even though Neela wasn't convinced about the idea of forming a duo, she was surprised that she never tired of it.

"Midi Mini," Neela countered.

"That's too 'RUK-MINI.' Not enough of you in there. Plus it sounds a bit like Minnie Mouse," she scoffed as she opened her Notes app where she documented their growing list of potential names.

"You should embrace it. Wear mouse ears in your videos."

"Sell them as merch? *R* on one ear, *M* on the other?" Rukmini jutted her teeth out and poked her index fingers above her head, looking more like a ravenous alien. Neela flashed her own teeth with a laugh.

"Exactly. How did you decide on your name anyways? The hyphen and caps."

"That was Puna's idea. She thought white people would have an easier time saying my name if it was split up."

"Well, your roommate seems to be right."

Rukmini's cover of "Every Song" had broken into the mainstream, with coverage in *Entertainment Weekly*, and her YouTube numbers were increasing by the thousands every week. Rukmini frequently reported the latest stats: "We're at 268K this week!" She always said "we" because, in her mind, this was their shared success, this was happening to both of them. Neela appreciated Rukmini's generosity and likely would have been bothered by its absence, but with every listen and every share, "Every Song" felt more like Rukmini's song and less like Neela's. Faced with this ongoing and uncontrollable transference, she was trying to let go, but the process of separating herself from her song, her work, felt foreign and uncomfortable. Unlike many artists, she had never considered herself a mere vessel for the muse, or a medium, or even a parent. Her songs weren't her "babies." Her songs were her.

Before she had listened to Rukmini's cover of "Every Song," Neela had always been able to fall asleep with ease. Once her head touched the pillow, the intimacy was so palpable that sleep felt like a passionate, seven-hour kiss. She would even wake up with her face slightly oily, like afterglow. In her recent state of insomnia, she wondered if choosing the title "Every Song" had sealed its fate. It could never be hers alone. As Neela had rolled from side to side between her silk sheets one night, a new internal voice emerged, a parental one that asked, *Don't you want*

what's best for the song? Don't you want the song to be heard?
She didn't resent the questions as much as she resented the
voice referring to *her* song as *the* song. When she got up
the following morning, she decided that perhaps silently
granting Rukmini partial ownership could be her way of
saying, *I will be your friend.*

"What a turnout! I'm so relieved," Rukmini said, as
the hall packed in around them.

"So brown too," Neela observed, appreciating all the
diasporic style — tikkas and lip gloss, sari blouses and
jeggings, turbans and bow ties, anklets and sneakers.

Rukmini handed Neela her phone. "You good with
this?"

with my girl @neeladevaki @swetshopboys show!
#pumped

The tweet included their new selfie. "Perfect."
"Shit, I forgot to tag the venue. How's this?"

with my girl @neeladevaki sweating for
@swetshopboys @thedanforthmh. come out
and play!

"Better."
"More personality, more chance of retweets. Don't
you think the Boys would love our album?"

As Neela retweeted Rukmini's tweet, she was con-
fused about Rukmini's reference to their "album." Was
she actually serious about this?

"So, would we write the songs together?" she asked, though what she wanted to know was whether Rukmini wrote songs. She reminded herself that if they were going to be friends, she would have to respect Rukmini's passion for singing covers, but she worried that directly asking about Rukmini's songwriting experience might suggest otherwise.

"Of course. We'd have to," Rukmini responded, dragging her Twitter notifications with her thumb.

She wanted to ask, "But how?" — not as an insult, but because she wasn't sure how they would approach collaboration — but she didn't press. Instead she joked, "What if you decide you want to go solo?"

"Oh, that will never happen. I'm barely even a solo artist now. Not like yo— oh shit." Rukmini pointed at her phone.

"Uh oh, who is Twitter telling us to be mad at today?"

"No, Sumi favourited my tweet!"

"That's nice."

"No, I feel bad that I didn't invite her. She asked me if I was going before you bought us the tickets."

"Oh. Just blame me when you see her at work." Neela shrugged.

Rukmini's attention was focused on her phone, thumbs ready to text the apology her brain was likely formulating. Then she looked up. "Can I ask you something? Why don't you ever like my photos?"

Neela almost let out a groan, but she clamped her teeth

together. Was there anything more banal than talking about the fictional world of social media?

"I'm not really into the whole social media artist self-branding thing, so I'm barely on Instagram." She lifted her heel and tried to seem preoccupied with the leather strap on her shoe.

"That's not true. I can see you like other photos," Rukmini asserted, waving her phone like evidence.

"Do you really want to talk about this?" She sweetened her voice like she was consoling a pouting child.

"Kind of?"

"Okay, fine." She dropped her foot. "I only like things I hate."

"You hate-like?"

"Yes. I treat the like button as a dislike button."

"Why?" Rukmini's crescendo of concern shifted back to her usual buoyant tone.

Tired of yelling over the house music, which had gotten progressively louder, and not wanting the people pressed around them to hear this embarrassing exchange, Neela pulled her phone out of her navy clutch and texted Rukmini her response.

If I like something, it feels kind of redundant and showy to declare it publicly. Neela signalled at her phone.

Ironic coming from a musician who is liked publicly *wink emoji*, Rukmini texted back.

Am I?

Rukmini texted an eye roll emoji.

I just think that actually liking something is a private, internal feeling. One that I relish. And if I'm going to be coerced into participating in like culture, I'd rather dispense these forced likes to the crooked photos or the ones that are accompanied by long melodramatic captions.

Hate-liking seems so unlike you tho.

I could say that about you and your tweets? Neela was starting to feel confined under her dress and regretted choosing long sleeves over short.

Which tweets??? Rukmini squeezed her eyes as though the brightness of her phone had dimmed.

A lot of them are cryptic. Why not just say what you mean?

"Ooooh," Rukmini said aloud then typed. lol u mean my subtweets

Yes

Sometimes it feels like the only way to talk about guys or yt people without worrying about the consequences, u kno?

Isn't that passive aggressive? Neela didn't know why she texted this. She understood what Rukmini was saying and agreed with her. She glanced up at the piano onstage and wished they were both inside it, their phones off and out of reach.

I see how it could seem that way but for me it's kind of an act of resistance

How so?

If I could just tell a man directly that he's being an ass-hole and trust that he would listen I would! Always a risk tho *upside down face emoji*

"Hmm," she said aloud, unconsciously emulating Rukmini. She waited to respond, watching Rukmini continue to text, her freshly painted aqua nails rippling up and down.

So I subtweet. I say what I need to say and move on. U should try it!

To signal an end to discussing this topic, Neela dropped her phone back into her purse and yelled in Rukmini's ear, "You've seen my tweets. I am pretty direct."

"But not with your likes!" This sounded accusatory — Rukmini also had to yell so that Neela could hear her — but her grin suggested otherwise.

"My hate-liking is an act of resistance too, okay? Rage Against the Algorithm." She was only half-kidding, but her comment made Rukmini laugh.

"No, but seriously! Sometimes I think brown girl subtweets are part of this secret language we have with each oth— Holy shit!"

"What?" Neela craned her neck to see if someone had walked onstage.

"I figured it out! We should call our band The Subtweet!"

"Would our songs be composed of subtweets? Very Carly Simon."

"Yes! Think of all the fun we could have! You could

even turn some of your Instagram hate into lyrics. Like, *Why are your selfies . . . so fucking blurryyyy.*"

Right as Rukmini shout-sang this line, the opening horns of the Swet Shop Boys' "T5" started to blare. She screamed and shook Neela's shoulders in excitement.

Recalling that night in her living room a week later, Neela stayed folded in child's pose longer than usual, mentally composing a tweet about how content she felt. Then she rolled up her yoga mat and headed to her laptop. As she began typing, she was arrested by a tweet in her feed.

Album by @RUKMINI's secret band debuts at #2 on iTunes

###

Rukmini woke up to a text from Neela.

Congratulations on your secret album.

Rukmini responded, ???

Neela texted back a *Billboard* link. The headline was a haze — except for the words "Subaltern Speaks" and "Hegemony." She turned off her phone and stared at the ceiling, spotted with glow-in-the-dark galaxy stickers left from the previous tenant. She thought about Malika.

She turned her phone back on and scrolled through her contacts, searching for Malika's name. She hadn't been able to bring herself to delete it. She typed, Did you see this? and included the link. Then she turned off her phone again to prevent herself from adding, I miss u.

Almost a decade ago, in the final year of her undergrad in women's studies, she had become obsessed with postcolonial feminist theory and, driven by her curiosity, she also became the kind of student who pored over the suggested readings in addition to the mandatory ones. "Keener," they had called her, but she fancied herself an enthusiast, a fan. It wasn't always the content itself that had appealed to her. She was infatuated with the *language* of theory, the way sentences expanded to include not one but several layered arguments. Theory didn't underestimate her capacity as a reader or a learner. Instead, it compelled her to slow down, instilled a patience so devout that it harkened back to the root of the word "patience" itself — *pati*, to undergo. Falling in love with theory had transformed her; it required her to let go of her skimming habit, to read each sentence over and over again, often aloud, until it unlocked and revealed its secrets. Falling in love with theory was not unlike falling in love with a human.

She had become so immersed in the language of theory that she began to recite from whichever book she was currently studying, even in public while she walked to and from campus, as though she was in close dialogue with the writer. Sometimes she would catch herself doing it during breaks in class.

Rukmini had noticed the other brown girl in her class who sat two rows in front of her, mesmerized by her dark-brown waterfall hair. Like Rukmini, she never went to the washroom or for a smoke during the breaks. Rukmini had made out that the girl's name was Malika from the mandatory name tent displayed on the edge of her desk, but they had never spoken to one another. This wasn't unusual — there was an unwritten code of silence amongst brown girls in white rooms. Staying separate was a way to assert their distinctiveness and delay the moment when their classmates or teacher would "accidentally" refer to one of them by the other's name.

Theory instigated the violation of this code.

"I am endlessly creating myself. I am endlessly creating myself," Rukmini murmured, curling her hair around her finger.

"Are you a poet?" Malika turned to look at Rukmini. Her face was the colour of fresh earth after a rainstorm.

"Sorry?" Even though no one else was in the room, Rukmini checked over her shoulder to confirm that Malika was speaking to her.

"I hear you all the time . . ."

"Oh. I'm sorry." Rukmini covered her mouth with her hand.

"Don't be. I like what you're doing."

"Those words aren't mine. They're from last week's Fanon reading."

"Right. Last week's reading. I'm still catching up from last month." Malika frowned and turned back around to face the front of the class.

They continued to talk to each other during subsequent breaks, though Malika never left her row, maintaining their territorial boundaries.

One afternoon, Rukmini pointed at Malika's iPod. "What are you listening to?" Small talk felt easier than asking Malika to sit next to her.

"Homework," Malika answered, shrugging her broad shoulders.

"Like an audiobook?"

"No, just something I put together for my music production class at Humber. It's due tonight."

"That's so cool! Can I listen?"

Malika placed her hand on her iPod as though she was telepathically asking for its permission and waiting for its response. After a drawn-out pause, Rukmini was about to interject and say, "No pressure, maybe some other time," when Malika finally reached over the desks between them and handed her iPod over.

Rukmini cautiously inserted the white earbuds in her ears. "A degree and night school? You must be exhausted." Thinking about her own evenings, she suddenly felt guilty for the hours she spent watching *Veronica Mars* and *The Hills*.

"Not really. Music is my caffeine."

Perhaps it was this metaphor that made Rukmini think of liquid as she listened to Malika's music. The sounds rippled and splashed, with liquid clarifying into stream, then expanding into ocean. She crossed her left leg over her right, anchoring her body and suppressing its urge to undulate. Malika stared at the round wall clock behind Rukmini for the duration of the track.

When the music stopped, Rukmini clutched the iPod, not wanting to let it go. "Wow. You made this?"

"I know. It could be better but I ran out of time." She retrieved her iPod and hid it away in her backpack.

"It's incredible. I felt like I was a ship on some kind of noble voyage."

Malika chuckled. "Like the *Titanic*?"

"Hmm. Imagine combining your music and theory?" Rukmini said.

At the beginning of their next class, Malika put her binder down next to Rukmini's and said, "Hi, I'm Malika."

"I know?"

"And you're Rukmini."

"That would be me!" She winked, not knowing how else to respond to Malika's forwardness.

"I think we should do it."

"Do what?"

"Work together. For the group presentation. Mix theory and music, like you suggested." Malika tore out a lined piece of paper from her binder, scribbled her contact information and passed it to Rukmini.

Each group was supposed to choose one article from the course syllabus and present an analysis to the class. They decided to meet every Wednesday night at Malika's place north of Dupont to dissect their selection, Gayatri Spivak's "Can the Subaltern Speak?"

"Wow! Your bedroom is like a studio," Rukmini exclaimed, tiptoeing around the black cables snaking across the carpet and the bumpy black foam lining the walls.

"I'd say that my studio is like a bedroom." Malika's correction made Rukmini realize that something was missing from the room.

"Where do you sleep?"

"That thing pulls out." Malika motioned at the black-and-white plaid couch under large Pretty Porky and Pissed Off and Desh Pardesh posters.

"That can't be comfortable." Rukmini drew her shoulders back, sympathy-cracking her spine.

Ignoring her comment, Malika placed a mic stand in front of Rukmini and adjusted it to her height. "Put these on," she said, handing Rukmini a pair of shredded headphones.

"Where did you get all of this equipment?" Rukmini spoke into the mic and then backed away. The mic smelled like raw onions. When Malika sat in front of her computer and turned her back, Rukmini exhaled over her shoulder, trying to smell her own breath to double-check that the scent was emanating from the mic and not her mouth.

"Craigslist mostly. The occasional garage sale."

"Really?"

"You'd be surprised what rich people get rid of."

As Malika clicked and typed in software Rukmini didn't recognize, she scanned the room. "Is that your sister?" Rukmini pointed at the small wood-framed photo of a young woman with chunky glasses on the couch side table.

Malika briefly glanced at the photograph and then

returned her focus to the computer, responding, "Cousin. But she's basically my sister. I don't have any siblings."

"Me neither," Rukmini sighed. She had often wondered how much her extroversion, her desire to connect, came from being an only child. "I'd love to meet your cousin."

Malika didn't look away from the screen. "You can't."

"Oh." Had she pried too much?

Malika swivelled her chair around. "No, I mean she's in the States. I see her once a year, if I'm lucky." Then she raised both of her thick eyebrows and asked, "Are you ready? Do you need a glass of water or anything?"

"I think I'm okay? What exactly am I supposed to do?" Rukmini bent down, reached inside her backpack and pulled out her highlighted photocopy of Spivak's article.

"Do what you were doing in class, but into the mic," Malika coached and then pressed Play.

Scanning the article quivering in her hand, she asked, "Which lines should I read?" while Malika's moody production filled her ears, distracting her.

"The ones that speak to you."

"In time with the music?" The soundscape was almost ambient with a barely audible beat.

"You're overthinking this." Malika got up and turned off the bedroom light. "Ignore the music for now. Ignore me."

The computer screen shone bright enough for Rukmini to read off her papers, but after a few minutes, she closed her eyes and let her memory move her mouth.

###

"Maybe this is a bad idea," Rukmini whispered to Malika as they shuffled down the stairs of the lecture theatre to the front of the room on the afternoon of their presentation.

"Just pretend we're in my room," Malika replied. She plugged the audio cable hanging on the side of the podium into her laptop and dimmed the classroom lights like she had done this before.

As Malika fastened the lapel mic to the strap of Rukmini's sundress, Rukmini looked up at her classmates. They seemed to have multiplied from this perspective and many of them had their heads down, already taking notes. What could they possibly be writing? She often suspected notetaking was more about *performing* engagement than actually engaging. But once Malika's beats burst through the mediocre sound system, their classmates were compelled to look up. Rukmini began to wish they hadn't stopped taking notes.

She stared down at the typed page in her hands and whispered the title, "Can the Subaltern Speak?" as though these cherished words were foreign to her. Seeing Malika nodding in her peripheral vision bolstered Rukmini's confidence, though she wished Malika was beside her. She said the title again and moved towards the centre of the room as she moved into the piece. Some of their classmates began nodding along with Malika, while also frowning, demonstrating how hard they were working to absorb the presentation.

Malika had built the track so that Spivak's words, spoken by Rukmini, were prerecorded. Rukmini recited their analysis of the article live in class over the instrumental breaks, ensuring a distinction between the theory parts of the song and their responses to it. But for the last eight bars of the song, the music dropped out and Rukmini assumed Spivak's voice live, quoting the line, "White men are saving brown women from brown men," acapella. The two white men in the front row resumed taking notes.

When the presentation ended, the classroom fell silent. It seemed as though everyone was waiting for what would come next. Rukmini looked back at Malika, standing behind the podium. Her eyes were wide. Rukmini finally leaned into the mic. "That's it?"

With this cue, the class cheered and whistled. When Rukmini and Malika hugged, the class cheered louder.

"We did it." Malika softly whispered in Rukmini's ear.

Rukmini and Malika continued to meet every Wednesday without ever making formal plans to do so. When Rukmini arrived at her house, Malika would play her newest beat or the latest effect she had learned in Ableton. Rukmini would listen attentively and ask technical questions, which Malika loved, like, "What is a hi-hat?" or "How did you distort that snare?" Eventually, she nicknamed Malika "Prof M."

"Don't your roommates mind?" she asked one night, as Malika cranked the volume knob.

"What? Nah. They're lucky," Malika shouted over the music. Rukmini dropped her mouth, pretending to be shocked by Malika's audacity, but she agreed. It *was* lucky to live in a house that brimmed with the energy of someone who was still searching, someone who electrified the walls and floors. Without Malika and her "noise," this would be just another house full of apathetic people. Malika's vigour made Rukmini rethink the idea of home as a place just for rest.

In the midst of one of Rukmini's informal production lessons, Malika announced, "We should form a spoken word pop group. Think about it. Nothing like that exists!"

"Everything already exists," Rukmini chided as she hit the yawn sample on Malika's sequencer.

"We could call ourselves 'Subaltern Speaks.'" Malika reached behind the sequencer and turned it off.

It was a catchy name, the kind that would intrigue Rukmini to check out the band. "But then what?" she asked.

"Keep doing what we're already doing."

"Why do we need a name for that?

"It just makes things official."

Rukmini didn't know what Malika meant by *things*, but she hoped she meant their friendship and she didn't want to say no to her new friend.

At first, Subaltern Speaks songs were composed largely of Rukmini's voice chanting favourite lines by theorists they loved — Sara Ahmed, Stuart Hall, Kimberlé Crenshaw.

"What about this one?" Rukmini got off Malika's couch and handed her a stapled essay, pointing at the line she had highlighted.

"How many times has this thing been photocopied?" Malika asked, squinting.

Rukmini grabbed the essay back and read the line aloud into the mic, "If you are free, you are not predictable . . ."

"Who said that?"

"June Jordan. The essay is called 'A New Politics of Sexuality.' We're reading it in my queer theory course."

"That's a solid quote. Lend me the article sometime?" Malika glanced back at her computer and then up at Rukmini, like she had solved an equation. "What if you tried . . . singing it?"

"Singing? I'm not a singer." Rukmini backed away from the mic.

"How do you know?"

"Because I don't sing? Unless we take that road trip to Detroit this summer. Then I'll treat you to my car voice."

"I just think these words are special. They were meant for more than just to be read or spoken. 'If you are free' . . . What's the rest of the line?" Malika reached for the essay.

Rukmini held on to it and read with emphasis, "You are not predictable and you are not controllable."

"Damn. What is she talking about here?"

"Bisexuality."

"Wow. See? These words need to soar. They can't be delivered in a predictable way. You have to sing them. Just try."

"Okay, fine." Rukmini sighed. "I'm going to do this because you've been right about everything else, but don't you dare laugh at me, Malika Imani. Now turn around." Malika jumped up from her chair and turned off the bedroom light. Then she opened one of the instrumental files in Ableton, hit Play and said, "Go for it."

Behind the mic, instead of closing her eyes, Rukmini stared at Malika's hair, trying to draw inspiration from the vitality that seemed to energize every curl. She began to chant the quote, as she usually did. But remembering what Malika had said, she tried to imagine what these words wanted to sound like musically. How might June Jordan have sung them? She began to lift her voice when she said the word *free*. After several repetitions, she had constructed a melody.

"I can't believe you just did that. That was incredible!" Malika cried, jumping off her chair again.

"You made me do it!" Rukmini buried the bottom half of her face under her Leave Britney Alone T-shirt.

"It was so effortless. You must have sung before."

"Not since grade school." Rukmini stepped away

from the mic, feeling guilty about her lack of training and experience, especially when she considered the hours Malika devoted to studying and practicing production. She also thought she sounded generic, like the one singer in a girl group whose name no one remembered. But Malika kept encouraging her to sing, and so she did.

For their final class project, they submitted a CD of theory-based songs called *Hegemony*, accompanied by an explanatory essay. They had taken several photos of themselves in Photo Booth and Malika selected the outtake of just their mouths, open in mid-laughter, for the cover. At their classmates' urging, they also posted a download link on the course message board.

Ten years later, that link and photo were everywhere.

###

It took Rukmini two days to respond to Neela's text.

In the past and with other friends, this delay wouldn't have been noteworthy. Unlike live conversation, text conversation was ephemeral. The connection could dissolve at any moment, without notice, if the lure of the text was not strong enough. Texting was sending a message in a bottle: all Neela could hope was that her message safely reached the other shore. Once perturbed by the medium's enabling of unreliability, she taught herself to appreciate read receipts, to try to find comfort in the word "Read" itself. *Read* below her "How are you?" text meant that the recipient knew that she was wondering about them. *Read* below her "Are you free next week?" text meant that the recipient knew that she was interested in spending time with them. She had learned to be satisfied with the knowledge that the person on the other end knew the intentions encrypted in her words. But Rukmini's consistent responses had retrained her low expectations. She was confident that every message sent to and *Read* by Rukmini would receive a reply.

This uncharacteristic radio silence worried her. Had someone in Rukmini's family been injured or died? But when she checked Rukmini's Twitter page, she saw that Rukmini had been retweeting all the news about the unearthing of *Hegemony*. Neela had composed many tweet responses in her drafts:

@RUKMINI I spent today digesting the album. Looking forward to discussing.

@RUKMINI Did you get my text? Are you ok?

@RUKMINI Time for Twitter but no time to text?

Rukmini's eventual response — Can you come over? — prevented Neela from resorting to Twitter.

When she arrived at Rukmini's house, empty-handed for the first time, the door opened before Neela could ring the doorbell.

"I saw you from the window. It's really nice to see you, Neel." Rukmini was holding a glass of water.

"It's good to see you too."

Rukmini handed Neela the glass and together they wordlessly walked through the house's smell of churros to her bedroom.

"Can you believe this whole thing?" Rukmini said, throwing herself onto her bed. Neela crossed her legs in her usual spot on the floor. She recalled the first few times she had visited Rukmini's place, how she had digested her aesthetic choices, stroked the spines of the books by Rupi Kaur, Gloria Anzaldúa and Angela Davis on her bookshelf and asked to see her childhood photo albums. Now Neela's fingers aimlessly fidgeted with the grey carpet.

"Not really. You told me you didn't write your own songs?" She framed the last sentence as a question so that she sounded curious instead of accusatory.

"I don't! That was a school project. It wasn't meant to be heard."

Neela had read that *Hegemony* had been recorded as part of a university assignment, with songs named after women of colour theorists. The original source of the album was a tweet from one of Rukmini's former classmates. This tweet had been retweeted 36K times. The louder the online noise about Rukmini's band grew, the louder the silence between Neela and Rukmini had resounded. Maybe this attention was what Rukmini had wanted all along, why she had been obsessed with the idea of forming a band with her, but had now lost interest. With their friendship weakened, Neela finally understood the comparison of internet marketing campaigns to viruses, the aspiration to *go viral* anxiously embedded in every link.

"Why put it up on the message board?"

"Our classmates asked us to! We never thought it would go anywhere. Our names aren't even mentioned on it." Rukmini spoke rapidly like she was still in shock.

"Just your band name."

"Yeah."

"Your other band . . ." Her mouth could not hold the words inside any longer.

"Oh my god, Neela. Are you mad?" Rukmini sprang off the bed and folded herself next to Neela.

"Mad? Why would I be mad? I'm happy for you. This is a big deal." She said these lines as smoothly as she had rehearsed them in her mind. And she meant them.

"What are you then?" Rukmini pulled Neela's hand off the carpet and held it in her own.

"I'm just a bit surprised. You have a band, and you have an album. I am not sure why you felt you had to hide any of that from me." Neela turned her head towards Rukmini's vinyl collection, noting how peculiar and even uncomfortable it felt to be in Rukmini's room without a soundtrack playing behind their voices. Without music, the room felt like thick emotion, like a clinic waiting room. She tugged at the cowl of her stone-grey shirt.

"I wasn't trying to hide anything from you. We were never an official band, and I honestly try not to think about that whole time. I don't even recognize the name of the person who leaked it!"

Neela pulled her hand back. "Then why did it take you two days to respond to my text?"

Rukmini curled her empty hand and sighed. Then she shimmied herself an inch closer to Neela, their knees now touching. "I was embarrassed. I look up to you so much, and I was worried you would listen to these old songs and think they were terrible."

Neela leaned back against the wall. "Well, I did listen to it."

"And?" Rukmini tugged the carpet now.

Neela had been unable to swallow all the buzzwords posturing as lyrics:

patriarchy
feminism
performativity
misogyny
white supremacy
gender binary
intersectionality
accountability

Critics had referred to the album as *radical*, another buzzword, and discussed the power of naming, but where was the artistry in merely reciting words? Hadn't Rukmini learned how to "show versus tell" in university?

"I loved the last song. It's different from the others," she offered, and faintly sang the hook,

Wanting is dangerous

"Oh, the bonus track. 'Wanting.'" Rukmini paused. "You sing it better than me."

"You sing it perfectly."

Rukmini reached over and hugged her, but Neela's body was still stiff. There was another question she needed to ask. "So what does Malika think about all of this?"

Neela had tried Googling Malika to hear what other music she had recorded and see what she looked like. But without a last name, it had been impossible to locate her.

Rukmini scrunched her face as though she was about to sneeze, but instead she began to cry. Before she'd arrived, Neela had anticipated how Rukmini would rave about how wonderful these past two days had been, how astonished and giddy she was about the online attention. Rukmini's unexpected tears were somehow comforting. She too had been distraught, at least in part because she was concerned about Neela's impression. Neela wiped Rukmini's cheek with her fingers, letting the salty liquid soak into her palm.

"I haven't heard from her," Rukmini stammered between sobs. "We haven't spoken in ten years."

###

"You know that girl who never said hi to me in the halls?" Malika asked.

"Vidya?" Rukmini responded. Vidya's disregard seemed to expand beyond the brown girl code of silence given that they'd been in many of the same classes.

"She actually talked to me today . . ." Malika paused on the sidewalk as the streetcar clanged by. They had said their goodbyes to their classmates after the commencement ceremony and were now heading to Malika's place for a private celebration of Jell-O shots and planning their Detroit trip.

"Really? When?" Rukmini gasped, clutching her new canvas purse embroidered with a pink elephant — Malika's graduation gift to her.

"This morning. In the washroom. Apparently, she downloaded *Hegemony*."

Rukmini cringed, anticipating a plunging critique. "Uh oh."

"No. She loved it. She said it helped her understand some of her course work better." Malika walked on, her stride almost a strut. "She even talked about connections she had made between the album and her Feminism and Film class."

"No way!" Rukmini playfully whacked Malika's arm.

"It's everywhere. Vidya said that she knew other POCs who had downloaded the album and felt the same way."

"Ooh, maybe we should introduce Vidya and her friends to Stacilyn," Rukmini joked. Stacilyn was a white girl in their class who had put up her hand to ask their professor if her presentation could be on Subaltern Speaks' presentation because she had been "so transformed by the capacity for music to disrupt and elucidate upon the formal page."

"No, but seriously, hearing all of this is more validating than any grade I have received."

"You're right. It's pretty special," Rukmini agreed. "I can't believe how many people are listening to this. I didn't think it would ever leave our class."

Malika stopped again. "Vidya gave me her number and asked me to let her know when our next show is."

"Our next show? Did you tell her that we're just a one-hit wonder?" Rukmini veered towards the Toronto Women's Bookstore, one of their favourite pit stops, trying to steer away from the disagreement that she and Malika had been having for weeks.

"But this is what I keep telling you!" Malika didn't move save for her hands that she motioned up and down like a lecturing parent. "We don't have to be. I sent the album to my cousin in the States and she said that people down there would lose their shit for us."

Rukmini was forced to turn around and walk back to her. "Okay but Mali, what I keep telling you is that I have 20K in student loans. I can't spend the next ten years living on instant soup and adding to my debt while we try to make a career out of some school project."

"How can you say that? How can you keep making jokes?"

"Being poor isn't a joke. None of this was supposed to be serious, right?" Rukmini lowered her voice, not wanting the other students walking by to hear them.

"It's serious to me. The impact that it's having. It means something to me. Why doesn't it mean anything to you?" Water pooling in her eyes, Malika tried to hide behind the curtains of hair fringing her face. Rukmini had never seen Malika cry before and, despite this argument, there was something beautiful about witnessing it. She had always believed that when someone allowed you to see them at their most vulnerable, the friendship was official. Taking a step closer, she gently drew back Malika's hair.

"Listen Mali, I love what we made. And I love making music with you."

"But? I know there's a fucking 'but' in there," Malika snapped and shook her mane.

Rukmini realized she had never seen Malika angry before either. "Mali, come on."

"Maybe it's best you don't come over."

"Really? Just because I don't want to be a rock star?"

"No, because you aren't who I thought you were." Malika glared an arrow at her.

"What is that supposed to mean? I'm still down to make music every so often. I just need to focus on getting a job right now, okay?"

"'Every so often'? Like this is a hobby? Don't bother."

"Fuck. Fine. You're upset. I get it. I'll call you tomorrow?"

Malika marched away. Rukmini raced to catch up with her, fighting against her high heels. Another street-car chugged by, taunting Rukmini. She had stupidly suggested they walk instead of hopping on public transit. They could have been tipsy and giggling right now.

"Mali, I am going to call you tomorrow and we are going to sort this out." She put her arm around Malika's shoulders as she caught her breath.

"No. Please don't. Please just leave me alone." Malika shrugged Rukmini's arm off her.

"You know, I always wondered if you even liked me or if this was always just about the music for you." As Rukmini's voice trembled, she turned away from Malika, embarrassed by her own tears forming. Through her wet haze, she could make out the lines of the university buildings, the place where they had met.

"If that's what you really want," she said when Malika refused to respond to her confession. Then she crossed the street alone.

She kept waiting to feel Malika's fingers tap her shoulder, hoping that Malika would have chased after her. When she gave up and turned around, Malika was long gone.

###

"You know that when someone says, 'Leave me alone,' they don't always want to be left alone, right?" Neela said after Rukmini finished telling her about the fight. They were both still huddled on Rukmini's bedroom floor, but she had finally stopped crying. "Sometimes 'leave me alone' just means 'I'm in pain right now.'"

"Of course I know that," Rukmini responded briskly, though she wasn't sure if she had known that then. "But showing up on her doorstep would have felt like crossing a boundary."

"So that was it? You just walked away?"

"No, I called her for weeks but she never picked up and she never called back."

Rukmini had also checked her email every hour, hoping to find a message from Malika. Eventually, the original purpose faded, but the habit persevered well into her late twenties.

Instead of wishing to hear from Malika, she began to hope for a message that would rip her out of her two washed-out black miniskirts and away from the hours she spent in heels collecting tips at Jack Astor's. As she earned enough to cover her bills and chip away at her student loan debt, she believed her escape, an invitation to a new possibility, would arrive in an email that she knew was on its way. She was sure that if she refreshed her inbox as a ritual on the five — 7:05, 8:05, 9:05 — even in the midst of taking orders at the restaurant, she could speed up the message's arrival. No such message ever appeared.

"You waited tables at Jack Astor's?"

"Yup," Rukmini answered, cringing. "The one on John."

"I can't imagine you working there, but I can imagine you being a great server. You're very personable," Neela said. She looked through Rukmini's bedroom window and stood up abruptly. "It's late. I should go."

"I can imagine you being a terrible server," Rukmini joked and was relieved when Neela's lips finally curved upwards. It had been a long night, but they were back in their familiar groove.

"Why? Because I hate everyone?"

"Pretty much. You would never master the FTT."

"FTT?" Neela whispered, careful not to wake up Puna as they drifted through the living room.

"The Female Tone Trinity. To woo the biggest tips you have to sound earnest, eager and coy." Rukmini emphasized the trinity by counting them out with her fingers.

"I'm guessing they didn't teach you that in Women's Studies?" Both of them cupped their mouths to muffle their giggles.

Neela opened the front door, letting the night air creep inside. Rukmini accompanied Neela to the honey lit road, and they hugged before Neela parted. "It's going to be okay," Neela said.

Rukmini leaned on the cast iron lamppost, watching Neela walk away. She promised to herself that this time she wouldn't fuck things up.

###

Dear Ms. RUK-MINI

I am writing to cordially extend you an offer for the opening slot in Hayley Trace's upcoming world tour. If you are interested, please respond as soon as possible with your availability for a phone meeting to discuss the details.

Sincerely,

Bart Gold
President, Gold & Platinum Entertainment

###

"Read it to me," Puna ordered when Rukmini showed her the invitation. Was this the email she had been waiting for since graduation?

"But you just read it yourself."

"I know, I know, but I want to hear the words out loud!" Puna leaped on Rukmini's bed and shrieked, "Hay-ley-Trace! Hay-ley-Fuck-ing-Trace!" Never snobby about her own or anyone else's music tastes, Puna had even fangirled when Rukmini had chosen a Justin Bieber song for her second YouTube cover.

Rukmini knew that she should have been jumping with Puna, but instead she was pacing. "Do you think Hayley would be okay with just me and not Subaltern Speaks? She does have a thing for alliteration," she noted, scrolling through Hayley's Spotify page, featuring "Daytime Drama," "Selfie Stick" and her biggest hit, "Hey! Hey! Hayley!"

"Of course! Bart emailed YOU! They want you."

"But I've never performed before," she said, still thinking about Malika nodding in her periphery during their one performance together.

"Isn't Neela a great performer? Just ask her to coach you," Puna suggested and then wrapped Rukmini in her arms. "I have to go to work, but I am so fucking proud of you."

After Puna left, Rukmini headed downstairs to the basement. It was hard to believe that a year ago, this makeshift studio, and everything that had followed since she had set it up, hadn't existed. Was this actually happening? Tired of scrutinizing the message on her phone, she clicked a screenshot and texted it to Sumi.

Maybe it's a mistake? Sumi responded five minutes later.

Given that skepticism was Sumi's default state, Rukmini shouldn't have been surprised by her reaction. And ever since the Swet Shop Boys show, she'd felt a chill between them.

Idk! Rukmini replied, spinning her office chair around.

don't respond. her music is kinda barf. it's not like ur going to do it. it's not a good look. for either of us lol.

Why was Sumi making this about her? How could she posture all the time when she liked Justin Timberlake?

does anyone say no to bart gold tho?

While Rukmini wasn't familiar with Hayley's music, it was ubiquitous enough that she wasn't entirely unfamiliar with it either. Someone had once commented on one of her YouTube covers: pls cover Hayley that would be amazing! But when she had looked up Hayley's music, she couldn't tell any of the songs apart. Even within a song, the verses and choruses seemed to blend together into four-minute raves. Rukmini didn't consider herself an authority on songwriting, but she found it hard to imagine a Hayley Trace w/ RUK-MINI show. And yet it hadn't occurred to her to decline.

Gold & Platinum Entertainment was the one of the largest artist management firms in the country, maybe the continent. Bart Gold worked with artists as big as Hayley and as indie cool as The Turn Arounds. He had a reputation in the industry for being a tastemaker, a younger Clive Davis–type, and musicians dreamed of being on his radar.

Sumi's response made her momentarily consider not telling Neela about Bart's message. Neela probably hated Hayley Trace too. But Rukmini didn't want Neela to think she was keeping another secret from her, so she texted her the screenshot and turned off the lights in her studio in wait.

Neela's text was polite: What a great opportunity.

Neela wasn't an exclamation mark person, but the absence of one at the end of that particular sentence was conspicuous. Was she being sarcastic?

Rukmini curled on to the rug by her desk and texted back.

I think Sumi thinks it's stupid or I'm selling out

Selling out how? We all have bills to pay.

But what if Hayley only invited me because I'm a "hip brown trans girl"?

Better you on that stage than another bearded white dude

"True," Rukmini said aloud.

Besides do you think if Sumi was offered a similar gig, she would turn it down? Neela continued.

Haha probably!!

Her loss. It's also hard to say no to Bart Gold.

Rukmini sat up and nodded. That's what I said!

I gave him my album years ago when I was looking for a manager.

No way!

Lifetimes ago. Let's celebrate when I come over tonight. 8 pm?

Since their conversation about *Hegemony* and Rukmini's past one month prior, they had been spending even more time together. It was as though they had each shed a layer of their defences in that conflict, stimulating the growth of a new layer of mutual affection. In one of her last visits, Neela had asked Rukmini if she could check out her studio and hear the covers she hadn't posted online instead of listening to records — like Rukmini was finally akin to any of the other artists they devoured. Reading Neela's texts, she became excited about the possibility of Neela coming along for part of the tour. They could hang out backstage. Maybe Neela would even join her onstage and they could perform "Every Song" as a duet. She wouldn't share these thoughts with Neela though. She knew it would sound like she was asking Neela to be a glorified groupie and Neela Devaki deserved her own damn tour.

Rukmini jaunted upstairs to the bathroom, balanced herself on the side of the bathtub and reached for the bottle of Lapis nail polish inside the drawer. She hummed the title line from "Hey! Hey! Hayley!" as she painted her nails, and then sang "hey, hey Rukmini" in the same melody, making herself giggle. Is that how Hayley would introduce her on stage every night? She giggled again. Why would *Hayley* introduce *her*?

As she flapped her hands to dry her nails, she became distracted by the braided fate line on her palm. When she had covered Neela's song, had she also accidentally stolen Neela's future? Distracted, her hand whacked the nail polish bottle over, and blue tears streamed down the side of the counter. Bart should have contacted Neela years ago, or even now. Maybe this was supposed to be Neela's tour. And yet, if Rukmini were offered the opportunity to return Neela's destiny to her, she wasn't sure she would.

She avoided the judging stare of her reflection across from her but couldn't dodge wondering about Malika's destiny. This was everything she had wanted. Maybe not performing for Hayley's audience, but performing their music for more than their classmates.

When the interview requests about *Hegemony* first started flooding in, Rukmini declined them all out of respect for Malika. Then she realized that she might be able to use the press to draw out Malika. Maybe one day Malika would be listening to NPR and, hearing Rukmini's voice and their old songs, feel compelled to respond to the text she had sent after their album resurfaced or the email she had sent to Malika's old university email address. She answered questions about their album in first-person singular, so it wouldn't appear as though she was speaking on behalf of Malika, but every response still felt incomplete, and therefore deceitful. Subaltern Speaks was so much more Malika than Rukmini — the whole band was her idea. Maybe this is why Malika still hadn't reached out.

Rukmini's online searches had also been futile. She had pictured her hand penetrating her computer screen, stretching into cyberspace and waving aimlessly, searching for her old friend. How lonely for the same hand to return empty from the land of infinite connectivity.

Where was she?

###

"You're here," Neela said as Rukmini stepped into her place, shivering. "I know your leather jacket is the look but it's no winter coat."

"Says who?" Rukmini chattered, snuggling her jacket.

A few weeks before the tour, Neela began to help Rukmini prepare for what would be her first shows and her first tour.

"Wow, it's so green in here. I wouldn't be able to keep a single one of these plants alive. Wait, is that an Amrita Sher-Gil?" Rukmini pointed at the large painting of three women hanging in Neela's living room.

"It is. You know her work?"

"I think I read about her in *The FADER*."

"The timeless tale of a brown female artist who is unrecognized until after death. And on that note," Neela strode to her piano, hit the C key and made a buzzing sound in tune with the note. "Now you try."

"Already? I kind of want to snoop through your things," Rukmini said, her eyes like a cat, zig-zagging all over the apartment.

"Maybe after. Let's stretch your voice first." Neela hit the key again to help herself focus. She too wanted to give Rukmini a tour of her place, point out her mementos and introduce her to her bookshelf.

"Fiiine." Rukmini flung her jacket on the matching couch and positioned herself across from Neela. She tried to make a similar buzzing sound, which quickly morphed into a giggle. "Sorry, I feel kind of silly."

"What, you've never buzzed with a friend before?" Neela joked. "If it helps, you can face the kitchen instead of me."

Rukmini shook her head. "No, this is good. Silly is good."

As Neela led Rukmini up and down different scales with hums and vowel sounds, she relished this opportunity to share her expertise. She also took pleasure in somersaulting through vocal warm-ups with someone else, especially as Rukmini's shyness wore off. She typically ran through them alone, before her shows, wherever rare privacy was accessible: in a crumbling hallway backstage, or a shit-stinking washroom, or even beside the dumpsters behind the venue.

"How do you feel now?"

"Like I'm rediscovering my voice." Rukmini wiped her brow with her forearm like she had just stepped off the treadmill. Neela took it as a compliment.

"Your voice is actually in good shape. But do some of these half an hour before your shows and you will be roaring. But hopefully it won't come to that." Neela circled around Rukmini into her sunny kitchen.

"What are you looking for, Neel?" Rukmini asked, following her.

Neela combed through a few vitamin bottles in the cupboard above her stove before securing the one she was looking for and placing it in Rukmini's palm. "Arnica. Best jet lag remedy."

"You are the best. Thank you for doing all of this for me."

"Well, you are going to be the best once I am through with you." Neela guided them to the kitchen table and sat down. Rukmini remained standing, twisting the bottle lid open and closed.

"Honestly, I'll be happy just not to get booed."

"Who's going to boo you?"

"Malika," Rukmini whispered and abruptly headed towards the door.

"Are you leaving?" Neela started to get up, but Rukmini returned with her canvas purse, stowing away the Arnica and pulling out a ripped piece of paper. She smoothed it onto the table, a map for the coming months.

"Sorry. I'm a bit scattered." Rukmini slumped into the chair across from Neela. "I'm still worried about not having Malika's permission." Her hand covered the list of song titles written in uppercase — her set list.

"For what?" Neela freed the list from under Rukmini's hand and scanned it. She knew that Rukmini would have to perform "Every Song" on the tour, but it was disorienting seeing her song title on someone else's set list. She briefly stroked her song with the tips of her fingers. She didn't have to guess how Malika would feel.

"For everything. This tour. Performing Subaltern Speaks songs," Rukmini responded.

"Did you run it by Bart?" Neela deflected.

"He said that as a co-writer, the songs are just as much mine as they are Malika's."

"That makes sense." Neela stood up and squeezed Rukmini's shoulders. "The tour invitation was addressed to *you*. Plus, you tried to contact her, and she didn't respond."

Rukmini placed her hand over one of Neela's. "You're right."

Neela found a red Sharpie in the stationary drawer under the cutlery drawer and lifted her chair to sit next to Rukmini. "Now let's get to business." She drew an arrow from where Rukmini had handwritten the Subaltern Speaks song "Wanting" in the middle of the set, to the end.

"'Wanting' is your closer. Just like on the album. Trust me."

"Good call. What else?"

"Swap one of the Subaltern songs for 'Sadness Is a Blessing.'"

"Really?" Rukmini took the Sharpie from Neela and wrote down "Lykke Li???"

"This is a pop crowd. They want to hear pop music," Neela said.

"Gotcha," she said, crossing out the question marks she had just written.

"Are you sure you don't want to use my rehearsal space some time? No one is using it right now," Neela offered. "I can come and watch. Give you constructive feedback?"

Rukmini squirmed and folded up her revised set list.

"You're sweet but I've been using my basement. And I'd be way too nervous performing in front of you!"

"Why? It's just me. Plus, we just mi-mi-mi-ed together for twenty minutes." Neela gently nudged Rukmini's rib with her elbow. "We have nothing left to hide now."

"I'm going to miss you!" Rukmini cried. She let go of her blush-pink suitcase and hugged Neela.

Instead of closing her eyes, Neela stared ahead at the flight information on the digital departures sign, checking that Rukmini wasn't going to be late for boarding. "I'm going to miss you too. I can't wait for the Toronto show."

Easing out of their embrace, Rukmini floated her hand down to hold Neela's. "Think about what I said about coming to one of the other East Coast shows? Or all of them?" Rukmini winked.

"You're going to be super busy." Neela glanced at the sign again.

"Sure, but I'll want to see you. And we'll talk every Sunday?"

"Every Sunday," Neela repeated and then let go of Rukmini's hand. Rukmini joined the security line of hoodies and jogging pants, already standing out like someone famous in her Hatecopy dress. "Go get 'em, Rukmini," Neela said to herself.

When Neela returned home, she sat across from Rukmini's chair and searched on her phone for the tour dates on Rukmini's website. She looked up again at the empty chair and sighed. Rukmini wouldn't sit there again for a long time. After she bookmarked the page, she noticed the start date for the tour and texted Rukmini.

Safe travels. PS I just saw that your first show is on Sunday. Don't worry about calling. We can talk on Monday?

Ok Neel! Can't wait to debrief! eee!

That Sunday, Neela woke up feeling bloated, nervous for Rukmini. She herself had toured many times but never on this scale — to that many cities and to that wide an audience. She patted her bedside table for her phone to send Rukmini a good luck text. She made the mistake of opening Instagram first.

Rukmini had posted a selfie with Kasi. With their hair braided, their heads were glued together with their tongues sticking out. Her caption said, If you don't know @KasiOnKeys, you will! She's joining me on the #HeyHeyHayleyTour

Kasi had posted the same selfie. Her caption said, So lucky to tour with this star. Come see us on #HeyHeyHayleyTour

Neela set down her phone as her pulse sped up. When had this happened?

Though the right time to introduce Kasi and Rukmini had never materialized, if Rukmini had talked to Neela about the possibility of having Kasi join her on tour, Neela would have encouraged the idea and arranged a meeting. Kasi wasn't just a skilled keyboardist, she was the woman you wanted on your team: she was reliable, punctual and had an instinctive understanding of when to offer ideas for collaboration and when to take direction.

Of course, she didn't expect Kasi to ask for her permission to go on tour with Rukmini. Gigs were how she made her money. Still, discovering this alliance between the two women in her life through a phone screen was unsettling. Their connection had been a secret — not from the general public, clearly, but from Neela. It also meant that, at some point, there was a conversation about *not telling* her.

"When will we tell Neela?" Kasi would have asked.

"I don't know if that's a good idea. She didn't react well to the news about Subaltern Speaks," Rukmini would have responded.

"She didn't?"

"No. She was *obsessed* with the idea of starting a band with me and was crushed when she found out I already had one."

"Oh."

"So imagine how she'll feel if we tell her about us."

"You're right. She would probably ask to join us."

Rukmini would have then cackled, which would have made Kasi howl, and after the tears from their laughter had dried, they would have agreed on the need for secrecy.

Why hadn't Rukmini asked Neela to be part of her tour band? Why had she chosen Kasi over her? Neela was not as good a keyboardist, but she could also play guitar.

Did Rukmini sense that she would have more fun on the road with Kasi than with her?

This must have been why Rukmini hadn't wanted to use Neela's rehearsal space. She pictured Kasi and Rukmini rehearsing for weeks in her basement while Puna watched and cheered. After they rehearsed, did they go up to Rukmini's room where Kasi sprawled on Neela's spot on the floor, listening to records and gabbing about music?

"You would hate being on that tour, Neela," she said to herself, pushing first her duvet and then herself off the bed. She was a musician, not an entertainer.

The next day, Rukmini posted a photo of herself and Kasi performing onstage in matching green satin jumpsuits. Kasi wasn't positioned behind Rukmini like a backing musician. Side by side, it looked like the two of them were performing together. A duo.

Feeling nauseous, Neela leaned against the kitchen counter waiting for the kettle to boil, her hand clamped over her mouth. How could they betray her like this? She imagined asking Rukmini this question. Rukmini would respond, "Betray is an interesting word choice." It's not as though they were trying to deliberately hurt Neela. Were they?

Neela tried to divert her emotions by thinking about Malika. She hoped Rukmini's original bandmate wouldn't see this photo. If she did, her hurt feelings would be more valid than Neela's.

When the kettle whistled louder than usual, it took Neela a moment to realize that the sound was actually her phone ringing. Seeing Rukmini's name, she considered not answering.

"Hello?"

"Neela! It's me. I'm so glad you're awake!"

She knew she was supposed to now say, "How did it go?" but that wasn't the question she wanted to ask.

"Last night was incredible!" Rukmini continued without prompting, her tone higher than usual. "Did you see the photos we posted? Did they blow your mind? We so wish you had been there."

Hearing these words, evidence that she had been missed and maybe not replaced, Neela's jaw softened. "Tell me everything," she said, hoping "everything" would include more details about Kasi.

"It's all a bit of a blur to be honest and I need to jump in the van, but I just wanted to call to tell you that the show went perfectly, thanks to you."

"You don't need to thank me. I had a lot of fun." Neela glanced over at Rukmini's chair.

"Same. Okay, I should go, but I'll call again later."

"Sounds good. Can't wait to find out more."

Neela soon regretted her words.

Once the tour was in full swing, Neela's feed was flooded with photos of Rukmini and Kasi, forcing her to flex her self-awareness and emotional micro-managing skills. She decided to commit all her focus on her transcribing work, instead of overthinking, but now, instead of the voices in the audio files she was transcribing, she heard her internal Rukmini voice engaging with a second internal voice: Kasi's. Together these voices had conversation after conversation, and in every one they were colluding against Neela. *Aperture*, *portraiture* and even *exposure* sounded like "don't tell her."

She then resolved to check Instagram only once a day, right before bed. This way, the surge of reminders of Rukmini and Kasi's fast friendship wouldn't affect her mood or ability to work during the day.

"Are you a Carrie, a Samantha, a Miranda or a Charlotte?" Rukmini had once asked when she and Neela had met for a picnic dinner in Trinity Bellwoods Park. The tattooed bros slacklining and licking charcoal soft serve ice cream around them were blessedly blurred out by the golden hour glow.

"I kind of hate that question."

"Why?" Rukmini sat up to face Neela, who was leaning against a cherry tree.

"It's the kind of question that women are supposed to sit around and ask each other."

"Yeah, because it's fun, and in my case, as a Charlotte . . ." Rukmini wobbled her head like a loose balloon. ". . . kind of embarrassing."

"But you're not a Charlotte," Neela argued, handing Rukmini the other half of her caprese sandwich.

"Well, I'm definitely not a Samantha."

"See what I mean though? I don't want to get sucked into this weird game where we project ourselves onto these white women tropes. Don't they do that to us enough in our day to day? Expect us to be like them?"

"Wow, shi gaw real," Rukmini said with her mouthful.

"You know what I mean. What would a brown *Sex and the City* look like? That's the question I'm more interested in."

Revising her Instagram schedule to nighttime inspired her subconscious to punish her with a vivid response to that question. Her insomnia was replaced by lengthy dreams about Rukmini, Kasi, Puna and another brown woman (she assumed this was Malika) going out for brunch, shopping and getting pedicures. Most recently, she had dreamt that the four of them went to the zoo together, but Neela was recast in the role of a caged elephant. Mourning the deterioration of her once invigorating dream life into literal-land in tandem with the tour, she adopted another approach — checking Instagram every other day.

But because Instagram's algorithm prioritized the most-liked posts, photos of Rukmini and Kasi appeared first and most frequently when she opened the app. She began to follow random nature photographers, hoping that a photo of a ruby-throated hummingbird or a maritime glacier would disrupt her feed and restore her calm.

When this strategy also failed, she briefly considered deleting the app, but she worried that this would be a sign of weakness. "I'm stronger than a fucking photo," she declared to her phone. But rather than prolong the war, her final tactic was surrender. Instead of looking away or looking less often, she looked more closely — at the numbers.

As she had been when she had noticed the difference between the number of Twitter followers she and Rukmini had, she was once again fascinated but this time by the astronomical like counts on Rukmini's photos. Many of the selfies that Rukmini posted looked identical — her signature cocked eyebrow, interchangeable hotel room setting and similar captions in the form of short love notes to the audience.

> Fun fact: the harder you dance, the louder I sing, the louder you cheer, the harder I love you. #reciprocity #HeyHeyHayleyTour

> I can't believe you knew all the words to Wanting. Can we please sing it together again tomorrow night? #comeback #HeyHeyHayleyTour #Hegemony #SubalternSpeaks

> To all the brown girls in the room tonight: you are my ultimate possibility models. You make it possible for me to be me #thanku #HeyHeyHayleyTour

Sometimes Rukmini posted a selfie with a different setting, the Eiffel Tower or backstage at the O2, but even in these photos, she wore her usual expression and included a love note. These captions were Rukmini at her most earnest and endearing, and initially it made sense to Neela that these posts were so well liked. But thirty sincere selfies later, Neela began to feel as though she had listened to her favourite song one too many times on repeat.

The thousands of people who liked these photos didn't agree. If anything, the number of likes was only increasing, suggesting that Rukmini's audience craved more of the same. Why was repetition so satisfying? Was the adoration simply a mindless craving for familiarity?

Occasionally, Rukmini's captions read more like subtweets.

> Hearing you babble through our set made me feel sorry for your date #stfu #HeyHeyHayleyTour

> I'm sorry you have never seen a breast before #deprived #depraved #getlost #HeyHeyHayleyTour

These selfies were liked even more (and admittedly Neela enjoyed them too).

But the measurable patterns were more troubling. She had noted a correlation between the increased frequency of Rukmini's online postings and the decreased frequency of her personal messages to her. Despite feeling rattled by the tour, she missed Rukmini, missed hearing the many observations she was surely making on the road. To mitigate her missing, and her hurt, Neela liked almost every photo Rukmini posted. The selfies that Neela couldn't force herself to like were the regrams Rukmini posted with her fans' comments.

So grateful to finally have a fierce brown role
model on stage! #queen #HeyHeyHayleyTour
#TransIsBeautiful

Saw @RUKMINI @ #HeyHeyHayleyTour and am finally
liberated. How did I survive before this? #whatatime

Some of the photos even featured fans wearing RUK-MINI mouse ears, posing with their awkwardly smiling brown parents. The images themselves were heartwarming, so Neela strained to pinpoint the real cause of her dismay. Was it that Rukmini had used her merch idea without thanking or crediting her? She eventually realized that neither the merch nor the photos were to blame. It was fans' repeated use of the word "finally."

"Finally" implied the end of disciplined, painful waiting through a drought and relief at the arrival of rain. Rukmini was her fans' nourishment, their cure. And she had indisputable gifts. But "finally" implied "only" — that Rukmini was their *only* nourishment, their *only* cure. "Finally" implied there were no others.

Rukmini had been performing her cover of "Every Song" on tour, but she had stopped tagging Neela when she posted links of her live performances on Twitter. Neela assumed this was because Rukmini ran out of characters to include her handle. But maybe now Rukmini really did believe the song was hers, and her fans, following her lead, thought the same.

A month after the tour began, Neela pulled the cleaning supplies and garbage bin out of the cupboard under her sink to unearth the old journals she had hidden there. She flipped through the lined pages, scouring for the handwritten lyrics that would confirm the song was hers. When she located the lyrics, written in her small fine print, she ripped the page out of the journal and taped it to her fridge.

Then, remembering the words of her yoga teacher — "When your emotions are in commotion, just find a floor" — she lay down on the pale parquet tiles. She basked in the midday lemon sunbeams bursting through the skylight, her legs stretched wide like a triangle. She was going to push the soles of her feet together into a diamond pose, but when her right hand grazed her thigh, it tingled. She slowly slid it until it was between her legs. She exhaled. As her fingers began to move, blood pulsed to and from every corner inside her. She moaned. Hearing the sound emerge from her throat and fill her apartment, she remembered the glory of her own body, her voice, her self.

After her pulse steadied, she grabbed one of the dish towels hanging from the stove behind her and wiped her hands and the sweat on her neck. Then she stood up, picked up her phone off the kitchen table and texted Rukmini.

I have an idea.

###

Rukmini was reapplying her lipstick in her vanity mirror when she heard her phone ding. From the corner of her eye, she could see a text from Neela. The word "idea." Her hand jittered and when she looked back at the mirror, she had streaked magenta above her lips. Before wiping it off, she picked up her phone.

Omg tell me!

OK. In person. Where are you? When are you back?

Telll meeeee!

"Fifteen minutes!" the tour manager announced, knocking on their dressing room door.

"Thank you," Rukmini said, fixing her lipstick. Then she mechanically checked her Instagram while she waited for Neela to respond. Her activity screen was a list of a dozen photos Neela had liked.

"Look at this!" Rukmini turned her phone towards Kasi.

Kasi glanced up from her own phone. "Aww, Neela loves you."

Rukmini frowned at her phone screen. "She's been favouriting all my tweets too."

"That's sweet," Kasi said, not catching Rukmini's tone. Before their set, Kasi preferred to be quiet and zone out.

"Is it? Or is she mocking me?" Rukmini seized the bag of salt and vinegar chips from the rest of their humble tour rider food spread — oranges, granola bars and iced tea.

"You're her best friend. Why would she mock you?" Kasi asked, putting down her phone.

"You know the whole hate-liking thing . . ." she said in between her urgent crunching and pointed the bag at Kasi.

Kasi shook her head at the bag and then at Rukmini. "Hate-liking?"

"I'm just being silly," Rukmini lied, realizing that maybe Kasi didn't know about Neela's online behaviour. She had been discovering that there was a lot Kasi didn't seem to know about Neela.

"You miss her. It's okay. I do too. I actually haven't heard from her since the tour started." Kasi got up from the shredded couch. "I wish she was here with us," she said before retreating into their private washroom.

She didn't share Kasi's wish. She was grateful that the Toronto show was still a few months away, giving her more time to perfect her set. She wanted Neela to see her at her best. She opened Twitter, browsed the latest hot takes and then tweeted, IRL like > online like.

"Rukmini, you ready?" Kasi was waiting for her at the door.

"Yup, coming," she said, stuffing her phone in one of her jumpsuit's ample pockets. As they climbed up the slim stairs to stage level, she tripped, but Kasi caught her.

"You okay? You seem distracted."

"I'm fine."

Behind the curtain, once they found a spot to stand safely amidst the cords slithering around their feet, Kasi put out her hands, palms up. Rukmini placed her hands on top of Kasi's, trying to tune out the house music, the bustling surly men with headsets and Neela's text. Next, they raised their arms and robotically twisted handfuls of air, imitating the white people who tried to bhangra during their Berlin set. Since then, this move had become a pre-show ritual, their ensuing laughter always bursting any nervousness.

This time Rukmini didn't laugh. As soon as they stopped, the backstage frenzy rushed in and Rukmini's thoughts cranked to eleven. What was Neela's idea? Was Neela going to record a visual album like Beyoncé? No, it would have to be something that hadn't been done before. Or maybe her idea wasn't music related. Was she going to write her memoir? Launch a photography exhibit? Compete in a triathlon? Why couldn't Rukmini generate ideas like this?

Rukmini felt her thigh vibrate. Sumi, not Neela, had texted her.

Can you hook D1 up with tickets to the Detroit show in May?

Why would Sumi ask for free tickets to a tour of an artist she had trashed? It's not like Sumi wanted to see Rukmini or see her perform. Ever since the tour began, Sumi's messages had fixated on Hayley.

So what's she like in person?

Can she even sing live?

Are you like bffs now?

The sarcastic tone of these texts reminded Rukmini

of Sumi's lack of support when she'd been invited on the tour, so she rarely responded. But they also stirred embarrassment about how little contact she had with Hayley.

"Well, that was weird," Kasi had whispered as they were leaving Hayley's dressing room after being introduced to her during the first week of tour. The spacious room was lit with only candles and Nag Champa incense burned in each corner.

"She's just a really busy woman." Rukmini defended Hayley to repress the part of herself that agreed with Kasi.

"But she didn't even turn around from her mirror to face us. It was kind of like we were her staff."

"Technically we are, aren't we?"

On some nights, as they sat at the main merch stand in the foyer after their set, catching only muffled songs and screams emanating from inside the venue where Hayley was performing, Rukmini replayed their brief brush with celebrity. She had always suspected that the tour offer was a diversity invitation, but she wanted to be wrong. She'd hoped Hayley was different, hoped that they would have pre-show dinners together and passionate discussions about production, inspiration and maybe even collaboration. What was it about whiteness that seemed to elicit an infinite spring of faith and second chances? But no such dinner ever took place.

Now side stage, Rukmini heard the background music fade out. The stage lights turned green. Her cue. The crowd screamed.

Sumi's text had made her think about having to return to her job at *Toronto Tops* after the tour, to the unpleasantness of writing corny listicles in her cubicle across from the ever-jammed and beeping photocopier. Sumi had probably been tasked a trivial assignment herself — writing about the show. Why wouldn't she just get *Toronto Tops* to comp the tickets? Rukmini shoved her phone back into her pocket.

"Get into the game, Rukmini. Remember how lucky you are," she whispered to herself, jumping up and down a couple of times. Kasi joined her. They walked onstage together, holding hands.

Kasi marched towards her keyboard and began playing the first notes of "Every Song."

Recalling that opening with this song had been Neela's idea, Rukmini's voice cracked.

"Aren't I just blowing my load by opening with my best known cover?" Rukmini had asked when they had discussed her set list in Neela's kitchen.

"That's how you win them over," Neela had advised. She was right.

The crowd didn't notice that her voice broke because she flipped her hair as it happened (another Neela idea: "just distract the audience if you make a mistake"). As she moved through the rest of the set, she obsessed over how many of her performance choices were Neela's ideas. Mid-set when she walked offstage briefly "to create suspense" — another Neela idea — she considered not going back on. Upon reaching their final song, "Wanting," she couldn't help but dedicate the closer to Neela.

"Y'all know Neela Devaki?" The crowd grew quiet and heads shook. "She wrote 'Every Song.'"

"I love 'Every Song,'" someone from the audience yelled.

"I love 'Every Song' too. And I love Neela Devaki, the woman who wrote it. She's the original. Go check her out. This one's for her." Neela, the luminous idea light bulb, and Rukmini, a shadow — or worse, a light-sucking black hole.

Rukmini croaked the opening lines of "Wanting."

Nobody can see my isolation
Nobody can see how much I want to be friends
Nobody can see my wanting
Don't want to be wanting

Her thoughts shifted to Malika, as they usually did during this song. During the first few shows, she had considered dedicating this song to Malika but worried saying her name would only draw more attention to her absence. She always half-expected to see Malika in the audience, her face even angrier than it had been the last time she'd seen her. Once she mistook a fan's sign for a protest sign, seeing only the *X*s and not the *O*s around "RUK-MINI," because the woman holding it reminded her of Malika.

Sooner or later, Malika would show up. Rukmini would stretch out her hand into the crowd and say, "This woman was my best friend in university. She taught me how to sing. I wouldn't be up here if it wasn't for her." A spotlight would shine on Malika as she floated onto the stage. They would embrace, and through tears they would sing their song together with the audience.

Because wanting is dangerous
Wanting is dangerous
I'll suppress the beast, I'll be my best for now

Or maybe Malika would snatch her mic. "Guess what, everybody? This woman," Malika would say, pointing at Rukmini, "this bitch doesn't give a fuck about friendship or music or dreams. She doesn't deserve this stage. All she ever cared about was herself."

Rukmini's mic almost fell out of her hands as she envisioned this scenario. Thankfully, their set was over. Rukmini hurried backstage.

"Are you sure you're okay?" Kasi asked, fanning herself with one hand.

"Your set was really good tonight," the sound technician interrupted.

But it wasn't their set. Or Rukmini's set. Wasn't it actually Neela Devaki's set? Or Malika's set?

"*Encore!*" the audience yelled, as every audience in every city on the tour had so far. Encores were uncommon for opening acts, but Rukmini sighed. She grabbed her bottle of water tucked between gear cases, gulped it down and then asked Kasi, "Do you think any of them are actually paying attention to the lyrics of these songs?"

Kasi finished retying her crisp leather boots, pushed herself up and responded, "Honestly, I've been wondering the same thing." Standing face to face with Rukmini, she placed her hands on her shoulders like a coach mid–pep talk. "Let's talk about this in our debrief after the show, okay?"

Then Kasi ran onstage and hit Play on her laptop, starting the instrumental she had replicated from the Subaltern Speaks' track "Audre." Rukmini followed and swayed, trying to replace her doubts with the memory of how thrilling it had felt at the beginning of the tour to sing and dance on giant stages. But after a few weeks, when she wasn't contending with guilt about Malika (and now Neela), she thought about how her experience as an opening act confirmed her discomfort as an audience member with their treatment. They were just that: an act. She wasn't an artist to Hayley, and perhaps to a segment of Hayley's audience. She was an impersonator or, worse, a stand-in, a nameless outline of a brown figure. Was all the audience's applause for her and Kasi, or for themselves for being so open-minded, so inclusive? Performing songs she had worked on almost a decade ago, songs composed of postcolonial theory, felt more and more dissonant.

As she spoke Audre Lorde's words over Malika's watery pads — "Your silence will not protect you" —

waves of enraptured white faces opened their mouths to release a collective shout. She knew this wasn't quite what Lorde had meant.

"So, who is 'Every Song' about?" Rukmini had leaned forward and whispered during their first coffee date.

"No one," Neela answered.

Rukmini sat back, disappointed. "Come on. There has to be a story there."

The story was that Neela's interest in her lovers inevitably declined into boredom. After the initial curiosity and desire to ravage one another physically wore down, coupledom was mostly an exercise in compromise. The beauty of singledom was never having to do the tedious and predictable dance of:

"What are you doing this weekend?"

"Depends on what you're doing this weekend."

"What do you feel like eating tonight?"

"I don't know. What do you feel like eating?"

At the core of "Every Song" was her longing for individual freedom. When she sang the lyrics *every song's about falling in love or breaking up / nobody's singing to me*, she knew listeners assumed either that she wanted to hear a song about loneliness or domestic ennui. But really, what she wanted was to hear a song that wasn't about romance or relationships at all.

The idea that had come to her in orgasm was to write that song — or rather to write an entire album of songs that focused on the thrill of solitude, the luxuriousness of her own company. She would call it *Selfhood*. She hoped this album would not only fulfill her desires as a listener but also bring her back to her own music and to herself.

When Neela explained her idea to Rukmini, she texted back immediately.

SO COOL. SO YOU.

Thank you, Rukmini *heart emoji*

She had wanted to hear Rukmini's voice when she explained the concept, but Rukmini seemed eager to know what it was right away.

And you're right, songs are always about love zzz. Or dancing. Or dancing in love LOL.

Not Subaltern Speaks' songs...

Haha. Don't remind me.

It took Neela almost three months to write and record *Selfhood*.

There was often a three to four year gap between her releases — an old-fashioned pace by today's standards. New albums and single releases were in her feed every day; she was repulsed by the vulgar tendency, particularly among younger artists, to vomit new — and often unedited — work rapidly. At first she had assumed this trend was narcissistic self-indulgence, or an addiction to the act of making announcements (as opposed to making art), the glee from bragging: "Look at what I am doing now! I'm amazing!" But after watching the musicians clamour for the mic at the North by Northeast panel she had moderated, she wondered if overproduction was a response to their fear that their value on the diversity stock market could plummet at any moment.

In the early stages of her own writing process, a song could swing in many directions. Making a decision about which path to follow required her to demo each song forty or more times, in different keys and at various speeds. Only when she had explored all the options could she be certain which melodies were worthy of saving and which to scrap. But with this project, she wanted to be less precious and more spontaneous — a little more like Rukmini.

Every day Neela would lie on the floor, as she had when inspiration first struck, but in different parts of her apartment. She waited for her thoughts and breathing to slow down. When her mind was clear, she would open her mouth and listen to the sounds that emerged. Inspired by her own name, she played with the possibilities of the vowels *E* and *A*, recording every permutation with her iPhone placed next to her head.

These droning sounds eventually pushed her off the floor and into her living room. Instead of sitting at her small upright wooden piano as she typically did when she wrote songs, she reached for her dad's old wooden harmonium, tucked on the bottom row of her bookshelf. He had given it to her when her parents had decided they were officially over the frigid climate and locals and moved back to Pakistan. Placing the instrument on her lap, she blew the dust off it and stroked the cracks that had developed on its sides from once-regular usage.

When she was a teenager, she had helped her dad carry this harmonium to and from the car every Sunday for puja at the local temple. This was the only time she had felt permitted to touch the instrument, which otherwise sat in their basement covered in a custom maroon-and-gold velvet case. Occasionally, before her parents got home from work, she would remove the case, put her right hand on the white keys and pump the bellows with her left hand, letting the sound saturate the room. Often she would just hold one chord, closing her eyes and swaying her head the way her dad did when he played. In this state of hypnosis, she felt less like she was pretending to be her dad and more like she was gaining insight into his mind and heart. Perhaps it was no surprise then that when she had played the harmonium, she pictured her mother.

Neela released the bellows from the metal fastener on the side, played her favourite chord, D minor, and continued to explore prolonged vowels. Twenty years later, she didn't picture her mother or her father as she played, but rather her teenage self full of secret musical fascination.

After a week, this process began to feel too hermetic and not reflective of her day-to-day independence outside her house. Feeling the urge to be outdoors, she walked down into the mushy valley of Riverdale Park, humming all the way to St. James Cemetery. In the company of bones and tombs anchored in stubborn ice, the melodies she sang grew more fragmented. She started springing between notes feverishly, as though it weren't safe to linger on any note for too long, simulating the dexterity essential for a single woman.

When she later listened to the dozens of voice memos she had recorded in the cemetery, the compositions were so shapeless that they sounded less like songs and more like what she would hear if she planted a microphone inside her chest.

She wanted the finished project to convey that same sense of intimacy, so she recorded the album entirely by herself in her home office, like Rukmini would, instead of turning to her regular collaborators for support as she had in the past.

"Wow, you nailed that take," her first producer had said from inside the control room when she was recording the lead vocals for "Every Song."

"Let's do it again."

"I don't think you need to, Miss One-Take Wonder." She shuddered, hearing the phrase "one-take wonder" come through her headphones. What was so remarkable about settling for your first attempt, about not at least trying to improve?

"No, I know I can do it better."

"Why don't you come in here and take a listen. I really think we've got it."

"Tim. I want to do it again," she asserted, leaning closer to the mic in case he hadn't heard her.

"Well, it's your money," he snapped, kicking one of the many empty Styrofoam cups strewn across the hardwood floor. Neela was certain that he didn't throw the empty coffee cups into the garbage just so that he had somewhere to channel his aggression when anyone disagreed with him. Sometimes she would purposefully challenge him, because nothing was more entertaining than watching a grown man throwing a temper tantrum as an intimidation tactic.

Eighteen takes later, her voice had taken a new shape, the low end almost a growl.

"I still think the first take was the best take. Your voice sounded prettier and sadder. Which is the right tone for a love song," Tim argued as they listened back to the track on the monitors.

The album version of the song featured the vocals she recorded on her twentieth take.

She thought about Tim now, about how glad she was that she wasn't working with him again and how vindicated he would feel if he knew that she was forcing herself to record her vocals only once. The difference this time wasn't that the first take was perfect, nor that she had grown complacent. The first take had the raw sound she sought for this project. Not overthought or overrehearsed. Another Rukmini influence.

As Rukmini's tour wore on, Neela heard from her less frequently. They couldn't compete with ever-changing time zones, jet lag, soundcheck and late shows. But they managed to chat on the phone every Sunday for at least ten minutes. It was never enough time, and after they hung up she often felt like an inmate Rukmini called in prison every week, disconnected from her real life. Neela was happy though to hear even briefly about Rukmini's adventures and then to return to her own album.

"When do I — to hear it?" Rukmini pressed this Sunday, as she had ever since Neela had told her about the album. "— sing — something!"

"Now? On the phone?" Neela cleared her throat instinctively but had no intention of singing.

"Or just send — rough mixes — !" Rukmini's voice was interrupted by what sounded like wind.

"I want you to hear it when it's fully mastered," Neela said, jotting down a reminder in her leather day planner to search for a local female mastering engineer.

"Don't — me — — dying to — !"

"Rukmini, you're cutting out. Don't worry though, you will be the first to hear it."

After she set a release date, she spent hours listening and relistening to the mixes at different volumes on her monitors, earbuds and internal computer speakers. She even rented a Camry for the necessary car stereo test to see how the album translated in another environment. As she left Toronto for Mississauga, her own vocals blaring through the speakers, she honed in on any flaws to berate herself. Why hadn't she sung the opening note an octave lower? Was the bass too quiet? She also tried to imagine she was a listener hearing these songs for the first time. What would she think? Would she make it past the first half? Would she listen to it more than once?

When the city's famous curvy twin towers, nick-named after Marilyn Monroe, began to loom in the distance, cutting through the fog, she unexpectedly thought of Kasi and parked the car on a side street. Onstage next to Kasi, she had always felt wonderous and indestructible. Would the buildings be as arresting if they weren't a duo? What would become of the buildings if they were split apart?

Neela reached into the backseat for the hoodie Kasi had loaned her on one of their tours a few years back. She had brought it in the hopes that dressing like someone whose musicality she admired would enable her to borrow their ears and hear what they heard. After she shimmied out of her wool coat, she pulled the royal blue sweater over her head and pictured Kasi listening to the album. How would they perform these songs live? Would Kasi even be available, or interested, amidst her hectic new schedule? She had considered sending Kasi the album, but their communication had broken when she had joined Rukmini on tour. Was it because Kasi felt guilty? If so, it was up to Kasi to take the initiative and make contact. And if she didn't reach out while she was on the road, Neela was sure they would sort it out once Kasi was home and they met face to face, like two professionals.

A few weeks after their phone call, Rukmini subtweeted,

TFW your bestie records a new album and won't let you listen #LOL

Neela sent her the album as soon as she saw the tweet. Rukmini didn't respond.

Rukmini couldn't stop listening to Neela's album.

Neela had sent her the unmastered files right before the tour headed back to the U.S. from Europe. Rukmini downloaded the files onto her phone as she boarded, grateful she had a long uninterrupted flight to give her friend's work the attention it deserved. She almost pulled out her journal on the plane to make notes, a holdover from her student days.

"What are you listening to?" Kasi had asked while she adjusted her eye mask.

"Oh, just a playlist," she lied, suspecting Neela hadn't sent Kasi the album yet.

She waited for the plane to lift off before hitting Play and then let Neela's voice carry her to the skies, unaware of her hands clawing her knees.

After she had listened to the first ten minutes, Rukmini's fingers relaxed. She'd worried that Neela, wanting to challenge herself, would explore the genre she loathed — electronic music. Before she had received the album, every time she sang over Malika's now-dated production at her shows, she had worried that Neela was simultaneously in her studio reinventing these very sounds, creating drums and synths of the future. Thankfully, Neela had continued to avoid the genre altogether.

She reclined her seat alongside Kasi, who had already dozed off, but with Neela's voice still in Rukmini's ears, she remained alert, staring out her window. How fitting to experience this music in proximity to masses of water and crystal. Unlike any of Neela's previous work, these songs were almost ambient, seamlessly mixed from one to the next. The tracks were named after vowels and had very few words. Ironically, these distinctive qualities also made *Selfhood* a quintessential Neela Devaki album.

The third or fourth time she listened to the album, Rukmini started to feel queasy. She poked at the compartmentalized chicken spinach pasta with her plastic fork but knew the food wasn't at fault. Suddenly, Neela reminded her of Malika — not her voice, but the way she channelled a talent so radiant that it illuminated Rukmini's shortcomings. She mentally replayed her fight with Malika after graduation, as she had over the years and more frequently since the resurfacing of *Hegemony*, trying to rewrite the past.

She wished she had said, "Fine. You want the truth? I'm definitely worried about getting a job with a useless arts degree. But what I'm more worried about is that the more we do this, the more you are going to see that you don't need me. You're the talent, the vision, the drive. You even made a singer out of me. You deserve a bandmate at your level. And we both know that isn't me."

She knew Malika would have retorted with "That's a fucking cop-out," but Rukmini would have been ready with her response. "It's not a cop-out. This isn't a hobby to me either, okay? But I'm afraid to invest more because I don't want to lose what we have right now."

Rukmini's re-creation always ended with Malika saying either "That makes no fucking sense" or with the ending Rukmini wished they could have had, the ending that would not have been an ending, where Malika said, "You can't lose what we have. And you can't lose me. You're stuck with me."

Then they would hug on the street and saunter to Malika's place, where they would write another song and another and another until their music blasted through this blip and trumpeted a future where they were still intact.

Except as she listened to Neela's album yet again, she felt as though Malika had never fully left. Instead her ghost had joined forces with Neela to remind Rukmini of her inferiority as a generic cover singer.

"So, what do you think of *Selfhood*?" she blurted to Kasi after they landed, hoping that maybe Kasi *had* heard the album and didn't share Rukmini's reverence. Maybe Kasi's opinion would console her.

"What do I think of what?" Kasi asked, stuffing her copy of *MOJO* in the side pocket of her duffel bag.

"Neela's new album?" Rukmini's stomach gurgled a cloud of garlic up her throat.

Kasi unbuckled her seat belt so she could face Rukmini directly. "Neela has a new album? Is that what you were listening to?"

Rukmini responded through her fingers. "Yeah. I'm sure she is going to send it to you soon."

"How is it?" Kasi asked quietly. Rukmini thought about lying. Not just to comfort Kasi, but both of them.

"It's very good." Rukmini's hand dropped from her mouth.

"Stupid question. Of course, it is." Kasi turned to face the aisle, hiding her expression from Rukmini.

After they disembarked in Atlanta, Kasi headed for the Oversize and Fragile carousel to collect her keyboard, while Rukmini waited for their bags. She turned her phone off airplane mode and was about to swipe past all the new notifications that popcorned onto her home screen when she noticed:

@sumimalhotra started following you

She and Sumi had started following each other on Instagram a week after meeting at *Toronto Tops*. When and why had Sumi unfollowed her? Was it after Rukmini hadn't texted her back about the Detroit show tickets?

And why refollow her now? Irritated, she was tempted to subtweet,

> can't get enough? eye roll emoji #follow #unfollow #follow

Instead, Neela's *Selfhood* melodies, which continued to waft through her mind, calmed her momentarily and then revived her agitation. She swiped away the Instagram notification and texted Neela.

> Hey just landed in Atlanta. Things a bit hectic. Can't talk on Sunday but will text about a makeup call soon! Miss you xo

By the time Kasi and Rukmini jumped into a cab to head to the venue, Neela still hadn't texted back even though they were now in the same time zone. Rukmini sucked in her breath and checked her Instagram account to see if Neela, perhaps now upset with her too because of how sporadically Rukmini was able to reach out, had also unfollowed her. She hadn't. Rukmini exhaled but she still didn't want to talk to Neela any time soon. Neela would first want to know what she thought of the album, and she would have to tell the truth, to offer her the word "masterpiece." And this would finally reveal to Neela the disparity in their skills, and ultimately in their relationship.

Rukmini was convinced that beneath the bed tracks of Neela's grand gesture to herself, *Selfhood* was a fuck you to friendship, and she wasn't ready to let Neela go.

###

On the morning of *Selfhood*'s release, Neela posted the album artwork — the album title and her initials in her fine handwriting on a white background — with links to the various music retail outlets on all her social media platforms. Then she logged out of each one. It seemed antithetical to the message of the album to pay attention to how others reacted to it. Instead, she strolled to the neighbourhood bakery, picked up a loaf of butter challah and whipped up French toast and a celebratory grapefruit and rosemary mimosa. "Cheers, Neela," she said, as she tipped the champagne flute against the air before taking a sip.

It was finally warm enough to keep her window open at night, and the smell of imminent green was intoxicating. Beguiled by the promise of fresh starts, Neela logged into Twitter as soon as she woke up the next morning. "Only four?" she blurted, when she saw the number of notifications. She clicked on her drafts folder to see if she had accidentally not posted her album announcement, but it was empty. And there on her profile, at the top of her tweets, was the post about *Selfhood*, retweeted four times. None of the retweets were from Rukmini. She told herself that it had only been twenty-four hours, that the response would grow, that not everyone lived on the internet. She also reminded herself that it didn't matter what anyone else thought. She knew she had made the best album of her career so far.

But the response didn't exactly grow — it fumbled. Every other week, someone would retweet her initial post or write an enthusiastic tweet but nothing like the response to Rukmini's cover of "Every Song." What made Rukmini's music more exceptional than Neela's? Given how close Neela's name was often positioned next to a number on Twitter, it was difficult not to seek answers from a number and not to equate her worth as a musician, as a woman, as a human, *with* a number. Thirteen retweets meant that thirteen people valued her work — and her. Being appreciated by thirteen people seemed like plenty, if not excessive when she pictured them as friends. But the number destablilized in relation to someone else's number. Thirteen was unequivocally less than the four million listeners who had streamed *Hegemony*. She imagined Rukmini crowd-surfing over four million people with heart eye emoji faces. Beloved. Quantifiably more than Neela. Neela $= 13$ and Rukmini $= 4,000,000$.

Two indie blogs had written complimentary posts but both focused on Rukmini. "So, has Rukmini heard the album?" the journalist from *Sheep & Goat* had asked over for the phone.

"I sent it to her, but she is on tour right now, so she's pretty busy."

"Do you think she'll like it?"

"I hope so. Some of my approach to this project was inspired by her," Neela offered, trying to sound generous to take her mind off the fact that she hadn't heard from Rukmini since she landed in the U.S. She had been concerned about Rukmini's state of mind, but her social media life continued to thrive. And unlike the past, Neela had been trying to trust that Rukmini would reach out when she had time for a prolonged conversation instead of a rushed catch up.

"Can you say more about how Rukmini inspires you?"

Even when she was promoting an album called *Selfhood*, she and Rukmini, or at least their careers, were seemingly inseparable. Or, rather, *her* career was now officially bound to Rukmini's. Maybe that was why Rukmini hadn't shared the album post or any of the related articles. Maybe Rukmini was tired of generating press for her.

She had planned to have an album release party, but given the response and Rukmini's and Kasi's absence, it seemed pointless. Was *Selfhood* a fraud at its core because of her desire to share it? Neela began to plunge into the wormhole that this question exposed, and she poured the extra bottle of champagne that she had bought for the party down the kitchen sink. If a self drops an album and no one hears it, does it make a sound?

Neela's salvation from this spiral arrived in an email.

Dear Ms. Neela Devaki,

We are inviting you to attend the upcoming Orion Prize ceremony.

The Orion Prize is an annual award that honours artists who produce music albums of excellence.

Her head tilted back and laughter burst from her lungs like a firecracker blazing through the fog of disappointment in her living room. Her star was being seen, at last. She opened iTunes and blasted *Selfhood*, listening and then crying with her eyes closed.

After a few minutes, she went to the Orion Prize homepage to find out when the shortlist and the longlist were being announced — the longlist not for another week, the shortlist a month later. This invitation had to mean that she had made it onto the shortlist. She returned to the message to digest the moment, to read and savour every line before she clicked Reply.

> We are inviting you to introduce the performance of 2018 Orion nominee Subaltern Speaks.
> Please keep this invitation and its contents confidential and RSVP by June 10, 2018. We sincerely hope you can make it.
>
> Best regards,
> The Orion Prize Jury

"Fuck." She slammed the computer shut and shot up.

Was this a joke? Wasn't it enough that Rukmini had stolen her song? Now the industry was finally acknowledging her existence by asking her to introduce Rukmini? Was she nothing more than a prologue to Rukmini's story? What about her story? Her years of hard work?

Then she thought about Rukmini and stopped pacing. Did Rukmini know about the nomination? She must have been contacted as well. She reopened her computer and went to Rukmini's Twitter page. She scrolled through Rukmini's tweets, looking for clues that she was aware of the news.

Why hadn't Rukmini told her? Or was this why she hadn't heard from her? Was Rukmini afraid that if they spoke she would break the confidentiality request? But she must have told Kasi. Who else had she told?

Guess what? Rukmini would have texted Puna.

OMG what now? Puna would have texted back.

I'm longlisted for the Orion Prize!

HOLY SHIT!!!

I know *shocked face emoji*

I think I'm going to come out to your next show *airplane emoji*

Really?

Absolutely! We have to celebrate this in person!

Kasi will be so excited to see you.

Should I invite Neela too?

Bad idea *zipped mouth emoji*

When Neela abandoned her inspection of Rukmini's tweets, she returned to the top of the page and looked into Rukmini's kohl-lined eyes in her profile photo. She hadn't changed the photo since the first time Neela had visited her page, almost a year ago. Neela's heartbeat slowed down and the thought of the fictional text exchange faded.

She picked up her phone off her desk and texted Rukmini.

> Orion. I am so happy for you. This is a big achievement.

She meant these words. Or wanted to mean them. The intention had to be what counted.

A week later, the longlist was announced, and her Twitter feed overflowed with congratulatory tweets for Rukmini from other Canadian musicians, including artists Neela admired.

> @jannarden: Hurrah for #Hegemony! So well deserved.

> @feistmusic: Big congratulations to @RUKMINI. Hegemony is a special album.

> @anjulie: Screaming! Subaltern Speaks on @OrionPrize longlist! You earned this girl.

Every *earn* and *deserve* stung, and Neela was surprised by how frequently and confidently these words were bestowed. How could all of these strangers measure the efforts of a nominee — and all of those who were not nominated? Did Neela not deserve? Had she not earned? She retweeted many of these messages to compensate for feeling sorry for herself, even though each share felt like an extraction, like something was being torn from her, hoping that this online support would inspire Rukmini to text her back. Rukmini remained silent.

Over the next few weeks, Rukmini continued to tweet about the Orion and to post tour photos. Neela began to analyze these photos more closely, trying to gain a better understanding of who was occupying Rukmini's time, who was more important to her than Neela. But aside from the selfies with Kasi, the photos were often a blur of smiling and screaming white faces behind Rukmini's own beaming face. Because of the flash, in many of the photos Rukmini's face didn't even look brown anymore.

It was the flash that finally gave Neela clarity, that illuminated the reason for Rukmini's silence. Immersed in so much white love from her fans, peers and the industry, Rukmini must have decided she no longer needed Neela. If anything, Neela was a hindrance, an anchor to Rukmini's origins. Letting Neela go was Rukmini's way of setting herself free.

Neela needed to be free too.

She rolled her neck from side to side. Then she went to her own Twitter page, clicked in the dialog box and began to type.

> Pandering to white people will get you everything
> #hegemony

###

*T*he moment Rukmini disappeared, I became more visible.

After my first experiment with subtweeting, I went to bed — stupidly. Rukmini had been right: subtweeting was unburdening. I had said what I wanted to say without directing my words at anyone in particular. I didn't have to say them to Rukmini, have to witness the wilting of her expression, the floundering of her words. And for the first time in months, I slept soundly past sunrise and late into the afternoon.

In my dreams, Rukmini responded to my original congratulatory texts about the award nomination via email instead of text, and her message was hidden in my spam folder. Certain that this dream was reality, that *of course* Rukmini had responded to me, I opened my inbox to search for it as soon as I woke up. I never got the chance.

My inbox was engorged with 458 Twitter notifications. Distracted by my dream, I had forgotten about my tweet. In the fifteen hours since I had posted it, it had been retweeted more than all of my previous tweets combined. Why was there suddenly so much interest in what I had to say, let alone in such an ambiguous tweet? Maybe including the hashtag of Subaltern Speaks' album title had been a little cheeky, a little pointed, but "hegemony" could also be read as a reference to the power of white supremacy.

I assumed that the online activity was mostly being generated by fragile right-wing white men who tend to have a hysterical response to any mention of "white people." Then I noticed that many of the circular profile photos in my mentions featured women of colour. Clicking on their profiles, I bit hard on my lip and scrolled through their bios and tweets, trying to figure out who these people were and why they were so invested in my tweet. Some of these women were young girls, students. Some were academics. Some even used Rukmini's photo as their profile photo and were seemingly fans.

"Fuck. Rukmini!" I blurted. Had she seen my tweet? I rushed to my profile page, deleted the tweet and shut down my computer.

Unable to walk away from my desk, I glared at the machine, my new enemy. Together we sat in a stalemate. Thirty minutes passed before I finally yielded — to my own guilty conscience. I turned my computer back on and stared at my phone in my lap, debating whether or not to text Rukmini. What would I even say?

Hello. I know we haven't spoken in a while, but did you see my subtweet last night?

Why draw her attention to the tweet if she hadn't

seen it? Perhaps I had managed to erase the tweet before it had caused any substantial damage. And if she had seen it, maybe that wouldn't be so bad. We had often talked about race and art, so the tweet wasn't exactly out of character. Maybe it would create an opportunity for us to finally reconnect.

This possibility was shattered when I logged back into Twitter and saw that the number of notifications had almost doubled in the past half hour.

Several users had taken screenshots of my now-deleted tweet. These screenshots were being tweeted and retweeted. I was tagged in every tweet. Credited.

Rukmini was also tagged in every tweet.

My legs twitched and my phone fell to the floor. Instead of bending sideways to pick it up, my body curled off the chair onto the hardwood and I knelt over the phone in child's pose. It took me a minute to find Rukmini's number because I kept accidentally searching under *N*, as though I was subconsciously trying to find my own name, so I could call myself in the past and say, "Don't do it." When I finally reached the *R*s, I listened as the phone dialled and repeated, "Please pick up," though part of me hoped she wouldn't. She didn't.

I stayed on the floor with my phone in hand and watched my words morph and proliferate in my notifications. Somewhere, Rukmini was also seeing these tweets accumulate. If she had to suffer through this, then, as the instigator, I had to too.

Every few minutes I clicked on Rukmini's actual pro-file to see if she had responded. Her last tweet remained the same — a photo of her leaning against Hayley's tour bus making a peace sign with her fingers.

I was woken up the next morning by a pinching ache along my left shoulder down to my lower back. I had fallen asleep on the floor, clutching my sweat-slicked phone. As I considered taking a shower to temporarily wash away the weight of my own shame, a respite I didn't deserve, I was tagged in another tweet — from @TorontoTops.

###

RUK-MINI UNCOVERED

Toronto Tops' *music writer Sumi Malhotra delves into recent Twitter controversy*

By Sumi Malhotra

When *Hegemony,* Orion nominee Subaltern Speaks' long-lost album, emerged last fall, the spotlight shone on the band's frontwoman, Rukmini (stylized RUK-MINI). While some journalists attempted and failed to reach the band's producer, Malika Imani, most writers and fans seem content just to celebrate the popular cover singer. In interviews about the album, Rukmini herself cautiously and cleverly dodges questions about Malika, focusing exclusively on her own process. On its own, this might seem unremarkable. However, upon further examination of Rukmini's rise to stardom, a concerning pattern of erasure of (dark-skinned) brown and Black women emerges.

Rukmini's big break arrived when she covered local icon Neela Devaki's track "Every Song." Initially this cover was perceived as a tribute, and evidence of the pair's then budding friendship on social media suggests that Neela happily received this gesture. However, the press soon stopped crediting Neela when they mentioned Rukmini's cover. In the recent *SPIN* feature on Rukmini, the word "cover" wasn't used at all, which implies that Rukmini wrote the song, an error she didn't bother to correct in the interview or when she shared it online.

To fully comprehend the politics of Rukmini's ascension, it is essential to examine the cover itself. While it certainly is a gripping, contemporary arrangement of Neela's song, the electronic backing combined with Rukmini's straightforward vocals pushes it into pop territory. This shift explains the widespread consumption of the cover: Rukmini's transformation has made the song sound, ironically, like every song on the radio. To date, there has been no acknowledgement of what has been lost. Neela's vocals and raw arrangement make the original version "almost unlistenable" (*Pitchfork*). This indigestible quality is arguably a consequence of Neela's brownness, and of the ways brownness continues to be alien, and therefore undesirable, in the music sphere. Rukmini renders Neela's work listenable by stripping the song of its original foreign, brown quality. This is likely what Neela was alluding to in her recent and widely debated subtweet: "Pandering to white people will get you everything #hegemony."

To examine the politics of Subaltern Speaks, it would be crucial to hear from Malika, the missing piece in the puzzle of Rukmini's rise to fame. Unfortunately, I recently discovered that Malika was killed in a 2011 texting and driving accident.

If she were still alive, would she condone the current dissemination of *Hegemony*? Sadly — and perhaps conveniently for Rukmini — we will never know.

I was able to locate Malika's cousin, Dr. Zuhur Imani, who is an associate professor of cultural studies at the University of Minnesota.

When did you first hear the Subaltern Speaks album, *Hegemony*?

Malika sent it to me soon after she made it, ten years ago. She was thinking about pursuing a career in music and wanted a close opinion.

What was your opinion of the album and her ambitions?

I told her the album was an essential addition to mixed media discourse being created by twenty-first century racialized women. I also told her that I would support her music career wholeheartedly.

Did Malika make any more music after *Hegemony*?

She recorded a few instrumentals that she shared with me, but she often complained about being unable to find another vocalist. She talked about the organic connection she and Rukmini had made and the impossibility of recreating this with someone else.

What has been your family's response to the resurfacing of this album?

It has been a process of both re-mourning and also rejoicing, especially as we witness the profound and impactful legacy of the work she has left behind.

Had you ever thought about distributing the album yourself?

No. Malika's passing was sudden and devastating. Sharing her class project was the last thing on my mind at the time. However, I am planning to teach *Hegemony* and some of her unreleased demos in my Word, Image, Sound class in the fall.

How do you feel about her "bandmate" RUK-MINI performing some of Subaltern Speaks' songs while opening for Hayley Trace?

Her performing the songs doesn't bother me. On the other hand, her profiting from the songs is extremely upsetting.

But the album is a free download.

Yes, but she is getting paid to be on a world tour with a mega pop star. It's also impossible to put a price on the cultural capital she has been accumulating from the resurgence of this album.

Have you been to any of the shows?

No.

I recently saw her show in Detroit and was uncomfortable seeing her perform these songs to a mostly white audience.

That was never the intention of those songs. When Malika shared the album with me, she was most stimulated by how the music enabled her to build community with women of colour.

What are your thoughts on the Orion nomination? Will you or anyone in your family be attending?

We were not invited, so we will not be attending.

Again, as with Neela, Malika's vital contribution as producer of *Hegemony* has been overlooked in most of the media coverage and by Rukmini herself, who has replaced her with Kasi Kamar (one of Devaki's former bandmates, no less) on Hayley Trace's world tour. As I mentioned in my conversation with Dr. Imani, my experience at the Detroit concert was troubling. Witnessing Rukmini singing these songs to an overwhelmingly white audience, many of whom recited the lyrics along with her, made me uncomfortable. It felt like a real-time display of sequential and sanctioned appropriation, beginning with the singer, passed down to the audience and then offered back to the singer.

Even more unsettling was the small population of visibly emotional brown teens in the audience who devotedly lined up against the stage. Their Instagram posts proclaim that they are grateful to "see [themselves] reflected" in Rukmini. This is the danger of an unexamined desire for representation. Is Rukmini the representation we need? What are the implications when a light-skinned brown woman replaces a dark-skinned bandmate with another light-skinned brown woman and, sporting the occasional cornrows, no less, is paid to perform the words of highly revered Black and brown female scholars for an audience of primarily white teenagers?

For the sake of transparency, I must note that Rukmini and I used to be colleagues here at *Toronto Tops*. While for some, the disclosure of this connection will undoubtedly reframe this article as an expression of my jealousy of Rukmini's success, I confess that my intentions are much more problematic — because they are personal.

As someone who has worked and even socialized with Rukmini, I am writing from a place of love. I am deeply invested in communities in which brown women support brown women. This is one of the reasons why I attended Rukmini's show and reached out to her at that time to speak to her directly about my concerns. She did not respond to my messages.

To be clear, the erasure of Black and brown women evident in this recent chapter of Rukmini's career isn't necessarily a result of her individual character or her duplicity. This isn't a call-out or an attack. Rather, this is an exposition of the ways we are all complicit in the maintenance of white supremacy, both in the music industry and beyond. My hope is that this article will remind racialized people that we need to stay vigilant in all of our practices so that collectively we can stop reproducing harm within our communities.

###

I am really sorry about the tweet. I deleted it as fast as I could. Please call me. I would love a chance to clear things up.

I don't know what came over me. You know I never do things like that. I wish we could just talk about this in person. Can you please call me?

I feel terrible. I wish I could take it back.
I had no idea that it would explode like
this. I am really so sorry.

I wasn't allowed to leave my apartment.

I banished myself. I didn't allow myself to reach for the optimism of a new day or summer air. Even after my hunger maliciously returned, I decided to starve myself, aided by my bare fridge. But after a few hours, not feeding my body felt like too easy a punishment. I had no right to wither away like a martyr or victim.

The absolution that I had predicted would come just from being outside started to wash over me, the midday breeze sweeping my skin as I walked to the corner store. I briefly gave in and raised my face to the sky. But when the burn of the sunbeams forced my head back down, I came face to face with Rukmini.

Toronto Tops had made Sumi's article — with Rukmini's face — its cover story.

"I want to take new press shots for the tour," Rukmini had mentioned the night she received the invitation from Bart, as we celebrated in her living room.

"That's a good idea. Which photographer are you thinking of hiring?"

Rukmini took a sip of the champagne I had brought over. We had immediately popped the cork. She clinked her flute against mine. "You, actually."

I put my glass down on the milk-crate coffee table. "Me? I'm not a photographer."

"But I love the photos you post on Instagram."

"You really should hire a professional. This tour is a big deal. And I barely post anything."

"Yes, but when you do, it always feels intentional. Not just when and how often you post, but the actual content and composition of the photos too." Rukmini grabbed her phone lying beside my glass and showed me my own account. "Look at the shadow of the sun on this building. You must have waited hours for the light to land like that."

"I think it's a great idea," Puna chimed in after she got home.

"You do?" I asked. I bit into the Spanish garlic shrimp Puna had brought from work and felt grateful to be spending time with her at last, instead of just pleasantly greeting each other in passing. She plopped herself next to us on their broad vintage loveseat.

"I do! Have either of you ever been photographed by another brown woman?"

Rukmini and I both shook our heads.

"What would that photo even look like?" Puna asked. The three of us briefly looked up in silence, as though we were trying to see a ghost.

The photo I had taken of Rukmini in her basement studio in the winter now gazed up at me, her eyes stabbing through the glass of the indigo newspaper box on the street corner. Initially I turned away, but then I made myself meet her stare. I knew she now saw the entirety of me, not just "friend Neela."

Despite the contents of the paper and the circumstances around the article, at first I was oddly comforted by the omnipresence of Rukmini's face plastered alongside the city's roads. It felt as though she was closer than she had been in half a year. She was home. She was everywhere.

But online, Rukmini's face was being severed from her name, and her name was being severed from her humanity. In the two days since its publication, Sumi's article had been retweeted 4,729 times. The retweets often included an assortment of hashtags directed at Rukmini:

#dragher
#coconut
#selfhater
#hayleysbitch
#subalternslut
#subalternstealer
#subalternsellout
#panderingpaki

How was this different than trolling? I continued to be tagged in many of these tweets. I wanted to tweet "please stop tagging me," but that would make me a hypocrite. This is what I had wanted, right? What I had been whining about? Not being properly acknowledged? My brain memorized these hashtags and scrolled through them in an endless digital loop when I closed my eyes at night, reviving my insomnia.

By midweek, I found myself prowling from box to box at one in the morning, slinging as many copies of the paper as I could find into garbage bags, an all too accurate metaphor for the damage my tweet had caused. If I couldn't control the internet, I could at least try to curtail the circulation of the in-print article.

After a week, I opened a *Toronto Tops* box and let out a quiet chuckle, relieved to see a pile of papers with a new cover story: "People's Patio Picks." I folded up my garbage bag and stuffed it into my back pocket, imagining Sumi's story also being stuffed down, buried by the latest news. I was half-right.

Sumi's article inspired several follow up op-eds and think-pieces where I was credited for

"calling out the anti-Black implications of Rukmini's interpolation of Black theorists' words in Subaltern Speaks' lyrics"
(*VICE*)

and was praised as

"an important example of a South Asian taking to task members of her own community"
(*Huffington Post*)

and even as

"a role model who is demonstrating crucial allyship in post-Trump North America"
(*TIME*)

Giving up on sleep, I vigorously cleaned my apartment in the middle of the night, burning my hands when

I scrubbed the tub, floors and counters without gloves. I listened to *Hegemony* loudly and obsessively through my headphones, the only way I could hear Rukmini's voice. I was disturbed by how many of Sumi's and the other writers' criticisms of Rukmini sounded like mutations of the very lyrics she was singing. How cruel that the language she had fallen in love with in university, that she had built music, a friendship and a career out of, was now being wielded against her.

Each time the song "bell" came on, I had to put down my sponge and hold still wherever I was in the apartment, haunted by Rukmini singing a fragment of a bell hooks quote: "How do we hold people accountable . . ." Her voice sounded on the brink of cracking when she sang that line, like a plea. The word *accountable* was also used copiously in many of the articles and tweets criticizing Rukmini, but none of the writers seemed to have a clear sense of how to answer bell's question. Every time the word appeared in my feed, I analyzed its usage, hoping to figure out how I too could be accountable — to Rukmini. Accountability sometimes meant:

@RUKMINI must apologize
(though it wasn't always clear to whom)

or

@RUKMINI should donate her revenue
(though again it wasn't always clear to whom, nor

did there seem to be a realistic understanding of what "revenue" for the average musician amounted to, let alone for an opening act)

or

@RUKMINI should stop singing
(though Subaltern Speaks songs weren't always specified).

The word *accountability* seemed to have a magical ability to elevate the veracity and status of the "writer" and the writing itself. Said writer was also not required to be accountable to the subject of their criticisms (by not using sexist and racist language to describe Rukmini, for instance) or to anyone else. One of the writers getting the most attention was a film critic named Vidya who asserted that the "lazy asshole" or "mean girl" (she didn't refer to Rukmini by name) had co-opted the idea to record a spoken-word pop album from her when they were in university together. She also claimed to have proof of this and, even without sharing it, her tweets amassed likes upon likes.

This blind backing made me switch from listening to *Hegemony* via the downloaded link to Spotify, a pathetic and belated attempt to show solidarity through stream numbers. But the more I listened to the album, the less I heard Rukmini and the more I heard Malika.

"She's going to text me back, isn't she?" Rukmini had

pleaded for reassurance through her tears in her bedroom last fall, after she had told me about their falling out.

"Of course, she will. The attention your album is receiving is Malika's dream come true," I offered, lifting a loose strand of her hair that had fallen on her cheek.

"The dream I prevented her from pursuing . . ."

"No one can be blamed for impeding someone else's dream. If Malika wanted to pursue music, she could have."

"Hmm," she said, leaning away and combing out the tiny knots at the back of her head with her fingers. "I just wish we could share this moment together. I wish things didn't end the way they did."

But someone else — a careless stranger — *did* impede Malika's dreams. How would Rukmini grieve the death of someone she had first lost long ago and now lost again? Even though I still hadn't heard from Kasi, I paused *Hegemony* and texted her.

How is Rukmini holding up?

I thought about how I had planned to take Rukmini to St. James Cemetery, where I had roamed and written *Selfhood*, when she returned home from the tour. I pictured her there now, without a gravestone to kneel before, weep at, knowing with certainty that she would never see or speak to or hold or apologize to or make music with her old friend ever again. Subaltern Speaks would never have a reunion tour and *Hegemony* was now a relic.

###

Hi Neela,

I'm reaching out to see if you would be available for a cover story for *Toronto Tops*. It will be a follow-up to our recent article about Rukmini. While your tweet has been extensively discussed and analyzed, this interview would offer you the opportunity to provide more context for your words.

Look forward to hearing from you.

Sumi Malhotra

Seeing Sumi's name in my mushrooming inbox felt surprisingly gratifying. Though she wasn't any more culpable for Rukmini's online dismemberment than I was, I was livid with her.

We had met once last fall at the AGO. Right as Rukmini and I had stepped into the gallery through the revolving doors, we ran into Sumi, who was on her way out.

"Sumi! What are you doing here?"

"What everyone is doing here? Looking at art," Sumi responded, looking outside.

"Ha!" Rukmini looked at me, her open smile trying to coax me to also smile. "I guess I meant are you here for work?"

"Nope." Continuing to avoid eye contact with either of us, Sumi reached into her pocket and checked something on her phone.

"Well, Neela, this is my good friend and colleague, Sumi. Sumi meet *the* Neela."

"Good to finally meet you. Rukmini has told me a lot about you." I considered waving my hand in front of her face instead of extending it towards her to get her attention.

"Nice to meet you too," she muttered, leaving my hand in the air. "I should get going though. I have a lunch meeting."

"Do you think I was standoffish?" Rukmini asked as we winded up the voluptuous wooden staircase, which was always the feature exhibition for me, the true crown jewel in the gallery. I often wished that the stairs would never stop curving, climbing upwards, like I was inside a growing tree that deserved to erupt beyond the building.

"You? What? Not at all. What was up with Sumi though?"

"She's always kind of like that. Actually, I meant to tell you. Our boss sent out this message to the *Toronto Tops* team congratulating me on the Hayley gig."

"That's nice of her."

"Yeah, it was. And so were all the excited responses from my co-workers." We paused in front of the lengthy curator's statement at the Georgia O'Keeffe exhibit. Neither of us were big O'Keeffe fans, but it had been almost a decade since the work of a female artist had been the main exhibit at the gallery, so we felt a responsibility to show our support.

"So, did Sumi respond?" I asked after we entered the Saturday-packed space.

"One guess," Rukmini whispered.

"You know, I really don't like her," I blurted. Seeing Rukmini surrounded by O'Keeffe's enormous water-colour flowers, it was clear that Sumi was a thorn.

"What? Really? Why not?"

"First of all, if that's what she's like all the time, she's rude. Second, she acts like she is this underground arts connoisseur. And guess what? She's just a journalist for a local weekly magazine."

"Ouch." Rukmini recoiled like O'Keeffe's *Abstraction* sculpture we had passed. I immediately put my hand on her shoulder.

"I didn't mean you! There is so much to you outside of that job."

"Is there?"

"Of course. You are about to go on a world tour! I just mean Sumi seems to think being a critic means she gets to be a dick. Including to her friends."

Now, months later, I was being offered a chance to confront Sumi directly. I imagined going to the *Toronto Tops* office to meet with her. "Are you so insecure about your career that you couldn't be happy for your friend?"

But then she would just retort, "That's rich, coming from you."

Rereading her email at my desk, I reconsidered meeting with her. I wasn't interested in "the opportunity to provide more context." I could barely recall the last time I had longed for an opportunity to provide more context for my art, let alone to discuss a subtweet. And even if I agreed to meet, but not for an interview, I didn't trust Sumi not to quote anything I said off the record.

Instead of responding, I created a filter in my inbox for any email with the words *interview* or *comment*, convinced that my continued silence, like Rukmini's, would eventually smother the media interest. But I still wanted to remain attentive to where and how this "discussion" was travelling, so I set up a Google Alert for my name. When I took breaks from transcribing, I scanned the articles the alert flagged. Seemingly frustrated by my refusal to comment on my motives or on the reactions to my tweet, journalists had begun to dig up and share quotes from old interviews that I had conducted with DIY blogs and lesser-known media outlets. Lyrics from *Selfhood*, the few that were there, were also scrutinized. The *Sheep & Goat* interview and review was finally published, with the headline:

SELFHOOD: The Neela–RUK-MINI Breakup Album You Didn't Know You Needed

This spawned stories about our supposed love affair, illustrated by our selfies together. Even my back catalogue began to receive airplay on radio stations across the country, particularly the original version of "Every Song."

When I received an email from Levi's about licensing the track for their upcoming summer campaign, I instinctively picked up the phone to text Rukmini.

You won't believe this. Levi's wants to use Every Song. Weird, right?

For a moment I forgot that Rukmini was no longer someone I could share news with. I forgot that any attention my music was receiving right now was directly linked to my disavowal of Rukmini.

As I deleted my text, the phone rang. Blocked number.

"Rukmini?" Had she been thinking about me in this moment too?

"Neela?"

I jumped up from my desk when I heard the sound of a man's voice and inspected my apartment as though he had broken in. "Who is this?"

"This is Bart Gold. So glad I got hold of you."

"Sorry. I'm not interested." Had Rukmini given him my number? I started to pull the phone away from my ear to hang up but I could hear him buzzing.

"No wait, I am not a telemarketer! I run a national music management company called Gold & Platinum Entertainment? I'm sure you've heard of us."

"I'm sorry I haven't."

Almost a decade ago, after my debut album had been out for months and had been only reviewed once, I decided to seek help. I had read a profile on Bart Gold in *Toronto Tops* and his "mandate to revive Canadian music with hidden gems," which inspired me to stroll into the Gold & Platinum Entertainment office on Spadina in my knee-high suede boots.

"Do you have an appointment?" Wearing a white camisole and with her hair in two braids, the receptionist looked like a high school summer student.

"No, but . . ."

"Well, Mr. Gold is a very busy ma—"

Right at that moment, Bart came out to the front desk sporting an ironed Broken Social Scene T-shirt.

"And who is this?"

"I'm Neela Devaki," I said and put out my hand.

"She doesn't have an appointment, Mr. Gold," the receptionist pouted.

"Well, I always have time for pleasant surprises."

Looking at the cluster of framed photos of Bart with Tragically Hip, Tea Party and Sam Roberts on his wall, I sighed, "Hidden gems . . ."

"I know. We have so much incredible and underrated talent in this country. I just want to help everyone. But first you. What can I do for you?" Bart spun side to side in his chair, legs open.

Sensing that this effort was a waste of time, I decided to get to the point. "I just put out a new album and —"

"Is that your album?" He reached over his desk and yanked the CD out of my hands. After listening for a couple of minutes and nodding out of time with the drums, he pressed Stop.

"Well, the good news is you have some talent."

I faked a smile. Great news.

"Your voice is not really what I expected from looking at you and the overall composition is a bit . . . niche."

"Niche?" Like a hole in a wall?

"That's not a bad thing. We could use it to our advantage. Are you from India?"

"No?" I started to button up my trench coat.

"I'm just thinking about the big picture. I could set you up with some hotshot local producers, get you doing some co-writing. I actually just signed an incredible guy — Marcus Young? Heard of him? He's going to be *huge*. I could set up a session with both of you."

I told him I would think about his offer and then did the exact opposite — until last year, when Rukmini texted me the screenshot of the invitation from him. I wondered then what might have happened if I had opted to work with him and Marcus and whoever else: Would I have been the one asked to open for Hayley Trace? Or was Rukmini the music industry machine getting the Brown Woman Musician equation right?

Hearing his real estate agent voice again on the phone, I knew I had made the right choice.

"Well, listen, I would love the chance to meet with you and talk about how we can support your career."

"Right now isn't a great time, to be honest." I picked up my house keys, jingled them loudly and headed outside, hoping the sound along with the outdoor noise would emphasize my busyness and disinterest.

"Right now is absolutely the right time! You have a fresh and authentic voice that audiences are clearly hungry for," he yelled.

"Oh, so you've listened to *Selfhood*?" I paused and leaned against a stop sign.

"Sorry?"

"My album? *Selfhood*?"

"Oh, I downloaded it last week and haven't had a chance to listen to it yet. Things have been so hectic in the office, you know?"

"I see." I rolled my eyes at my reflection in the window of a car braked beside me.

"But everything you have been saying online is exactly the kind of commentary this industry needs. You are the kind of hidden gem that made me start G&P."

I agreed to meet with Bart (another lie — the only way to get him off the phone), and appreciating the humidity, I continued walking west, past Riverside Bridge, and then turned off the main strip, back onto the residential streets. Bart's persistence made me think about Sumi, how her approach with her interview request a few weeks ago had been the opposite — short and no follow-up message. Unless my inbox had filtered her messages out.

It turned out that Sumi had just moved on. Lying on the sidewalk at the foot of the steps of a church was the latest issue of *Toronto Tops*.

The cover featured another face I recognized.

###

HAYLEY SPEAKS

Exclusive interview with pop star Hayley Trace
By Sumi Malhotra

Where were you when you saw Neela Devaki's subtweet?

Honestly, I didn't see it until a few days after it was posted, and by then it had already been deleted. My manager Bart Gold texted me a screenshot.

Did you know it was directed at Rukmini?

I had no idea what it was about. It's a subtweet. Who has the time to analyze all the weird stuff that gets said on the internet? But Bart kind of explained it to me.

And what did you think about it then?

Well, my job as a cis straight white woman is not really to weigh in on a dispute between brown women. My job as an ally is to amplify and support, which is why I invited Rukmini on the tour to begin with and why I immediately checked in with Rukmini after I saw the tweet.

What was Rukmini's response?

She seemed fine. Quiet, but fine. She's a trooper.

Where is she now?

I'm not sure. I assume back in Toronto? It's so hard to keep track of everyone's comings and goings on the tour.

It's been over a month now since Neela's tweet. During part of this time, your tour was on a scheduled break, but I see that some recent and upcoming dates have been postponed. Is this connected to the controversy surrounding Rukmini or the comments made by Malika's cousin?

No, I've been under a lot of stress running a massive show night after night and my physician prescribed immediate bed rest.

I do want to go on the record to say that I never endorsed Rukmini's decision to perform Subaltern Speaks songs on my tour. Nor did my management company, Gold & Platinum Entertainment. She was invited as a solo artist.

That said, I am deeply concerned about the impact all of this is having on Rukmini and I am not sure that continuing this tour together makes the most sense for her at this time.

So is the tour ending?

Definitely not! But we have suggested that Rukmini take a break from the tour. She probably needs it more than I do.

When will she be rejoining you?

I don't know. It's a bit up in the air right now. But I do know that the upcoming shows are going to be spectacular. I am launching a new single, and we have hired more dancers and another lighting designer. There's a lot to look forward to!

###

That bitch Hayley Trace kicked Rukmini off her tour.

I chucked the paper back on the pavement where I had found it and darted back home.

I had assumed Hayley's management would advise her to do the opposite, given that "all press is good press." Wasn't all of this great publicity for the tour? And yet, Hayley's decision also wasn't surprising. She had squeezed what she wanted out of Rukmini — underground cred and a badge on her allyship card — and could now toss her aside like a dried-up piece of fruit. One way or another, white people always found a way to fuck a brown woman over.

The more I thought about this and about Hayley's interview, the more I knew I could no longer afford to remain silent. I had to do something. Noticing the posters wheat-pasted to the boards surrounding a construction site, I wondered about making a bold declaration online.

When I returned home, I paced around my living room with my phone in my hand, brainstorming ideas in the Notes app.

— Publicly apologize to Rukmini

How do you apologize for a subtweet? "I'm sorry I implied Rukmini was pandering to white people"? Would that do much more for Rukmini than my personal apologies had?

— Publicly defend Rukmini

But what if my statement backfired and somehow heightened the animosity towards Rukmini?

— Call for a boycott of Toronto Tops and/or Sumi Malhotra and/or Hayley Trace for character defamation

No, that would only give them more attention.

— Write an op-ed with an invented narrative about how challenging Rukmini's childhood had been and how hard she has worked to persevere

Obviously, this was a bad idea, but it seemed the performance of pain on the internet was often a successful means of eliciting sympathy (and popularity).

Was silence the best option, or just the easiest? I closed the Notes app and remembered how often Rukmini had used it to compile our list of potential band names. Had she deleted that note now?

My index finger slid to my Photos folder and I scrolled longingly through photos that Rukmini and I had taken together. I stopped at the selfie from the Swet Shop Boys show with the piano onstage behind us and sank into my couch. I remembered how seen I had felt when Rukmini told me that she could imagine me living amongst the black-and-white keys. I wished we could go back to that moment, the discovering-each-other phase, the addictive self-revelation-through-another's-eyes phase.

That was also the night we had first talked about subtweeting.

Sometimes I think brown girl subtweets are part of this secret language we have with each other.

Rukmini's words haunted me as I flipped through the rest of our photos, landing on the selfie we had taken at the end of our first coffee date. After mentally weighing the pros and cons, I opened my Twitter app and tweeted,

No matter what anyone says, the real tea is served on Saturday afternoons.

That Saturday, I arrived at Grapefruit Moon at 11:30 a.m., wishing I had mentioned a specific time in my new subtweet. As I feared, the tweet attracted attention and was retweeted 214 times. My followers — who had quadrupled in number since I first met Rukmini — speculated that I was finally going to make some kind of public statement on Saturday. I hoped that every retweet increased the chance that Rukmini would see it and decrypt my code. Sitting in the café, I suddenly felt confident that Rukmini would show up. I had no idea if she was even in town, let alone ready to meet with me, but being back at our old spot felt right. If this were a movie, if there was to be a reunion, if we were to repair our friendship, this was where it would happen.

That was likely why I had spent over an hour trying to

decide what to wear. Combing through my closet, I had agonized over what clothing (and then what makeup) would help me appear both friendly and remorseful without seeming overly staged. In the end, I had decided to tie my hair up and wear jeans and a T-shirt — echoing Rukmini's look from the first time we met — assuming that she might feel most comfortable in the company of a version of herself.

"Sorry to keep you waiting. We are a bit understaffed at the moment. What can I get for you?" the server asked.

"Two peppermint teas with agave."

After forty minutes passed and the teas had gotten cold, the server returned. "Is your friend coming?"

"I hope so."

"Do you mind if we move you to the bar for now? Saturday brunch is a pretty busy time for us and we can't afford to lose a whole table."

I ordered an omelette from the chef flipping and grilling on the other side of the bar to fill the time. I ate every bite slowly, chewing the prescribed ten times before swallowing, distracting myself from staring at the door. I remembered the first time we were supposed to meet, how I had almost stood her up. Maybe it would be fitting if Rukmini didn't show up.

After I had eaten everything on my plate including the parsley garnish, I reached for my phone, bouncing between my inbox, my texts and Twitter, in case Rukmini had sent me a message. At around 2 p.m. some of my followers began to lose their patience:

At 3 p.m., the server took pity on me and moved me back to a table. Feeling equally embarrassed, I ordered the squash soup. At around 6 p.m., I paid the bill, left a large tip and trudged out of the café alone, half-expecting to look up and see the rain clouds that this sad scene called for.

Maybe Rukmini hadn't seen my tweet. Maybe she wasn't even in the city. Or maybe she was holed up in her basement, channelling her feelings into new music while Puna doted on her. The image of her studio unconsciously steered me from the café south to Rukmini's house on Palmerston and compelled my finger to press the doorbell.

"She's not here," Puna said, barely opening the door.

"Can you tell her I stopped by? And can you give her this?" I pulled out the folded envelope I had tucked into my inside jacket pocket that morning. I had brought it with me to the café in case my spoken words didn't convey everything I wanted to say.

Puna reluctantly opened the door and took the letter. I tried to glance behind her to see if Rukmini was there, but Puna deliberately moved her head directly into my sight line.

"You know, all she wanted was for you to like her."

"But of course, I like her. I lov—"

"No, as her peer. To actually respect her."

On the streetcar back to my place, gripping the metal bar overhead, I couldn't stop thinking about Puna's words. Had I never shown Rukmini that I respected her?

###

Dear Rukmini,

I'm writing this letter because I owe you more than an apology. I owe you an admission:

I was jealous.

Maybe if I had admitted this to myself sooner, I wouldn't have reacted the way I did. But contrary to what has been suggested, it wasn't the award nomination, the tour, the press or the praise that made me jealous. I was jealous of your effortlessness (or rather, of how easy you made it all look, at least to me).

Like thousands of other artists, I believed if I didn't bleed in the creation process, I wasn't making art. It was easy for me to devalue or ignore commercial art, however successful it was, because commercial art was easy, bloodless. It was meant for a lazy audience uninterested in blood. They wanted watered-down fountain pop.

But then you showed up. You took something of mine, something I built from scratch, and remodelled it. You refined it, while preserving my bloodstains. You enhanced the song's emotionality while making it danceable.

Watching your cover achieve both fringe and mainstream success, I wasn't able to easily dismiss the art — because it was partially mine. I wasn't able to discredit you either. To my surprise, I loved it.

This realization forced me to reexamine (and eventually ravage) my entire artistic framework. Had I been wrong in my extremism this whole time? You never seemed consumed by the weight of discipline or precision. Instead you created from a place of curiosity. For you, art was exploration, not excavation. And this was what made me most jealous.

Do you remember that afternoon when you opened up Ableton to show me how you had built "Every Song"? I was so unsettled by how disorganized the project looked. None of the tracks had been labelled or colour-coded, and some of the drum tracks were placed in between the vocal tracks. But I was more unsettled by how little this mattered to the final result. How could such beauty be born from such disarray? Or was this precisely the magic behind your work?

You approached our friendship with the same sort of haphazard enthusiasm and wonder. You had questions and ideas and opinions. All I had were my regulations and reservations. But unlike most, you didn't see these qualities as stuffiness or me as standoffish. You understood that, for brown women in a white world, self-preservation takes many forms. And similarly, I began to see your qualities not as immaturity or flippancy, but as a different form of self-preservation. You thrived on building connections with other brown women. And yet, when you and Kasi became friends, again I was jealous of your ability to open up so freely to someone new, when it had taken me so long to open up to you.

During these past few months, I have often looked for a green-eyed monster in the mirror and have been disappointed to see my own face. Seeing (and then hating) myself as a monster would be relatively easy. Instead, I am recognizing that the real monstrosity is not in wanting — even if it's wanting what someone you love possesses — but in harbouring jealousy without naming it.

So I am writing it down here in hopes that I never make this mistake again, and that it's not too late.

I miss you.

Neela

###

Once I reached my apartment, I planned on adding a few more sentences to address what Puna had shared. I would then try to find Puna's email address online, send her the revised version and ask her to swap the revised letter. Maybe that was asking too much from Puna. Maybe I would just go back to Rukmini's house and hand-deliver the replacement.

My planning was interrupted by an unexpected visitor sitting on the steps outside my house.

###

"Oh I'm so happy to see you, Neels," she said, throwing her arms around me.

"You are?"

"Of course, I am."

"Even after what I did?"

"What you did . . ."

"I know. It was vile," I admitted, waiting to be berated, at last.

"No, it was necessary."

"Oh, Kasi. Not you too?"

"We've so much to talk about. Can I come in?"

Seeing Kasi in my apartment, watching her fingers lightly trail along my piano, brought back memories of rehearsing for shows, rearranging album songs so they would soar in a live performance and going over set lists. I'd forgotten how short she was, how my leather couch cocooned her. She looked as though she was going to fall asleep right there, but instead she picked up what she had started outside.

"Those shows. That tour. It was so hard. On both of us."

"It looked like you were both having the time of your lives," I interjected, pulling the bench from under the piano, Kasi's usual spot in my house, and sitting on it across from her. I needed to be able to see her expressions to get full clarity after all the months we hadn't spoken. I was done with internet ambiguities.

"That's the point of social media, isn't it?" Kasi stretched her eyes and mouth in an exaggerated smile, looking like a vacant clown.

"I suppose?"

Kasi reached for my hand and once I gave it to her, she tugged on it to help her sit upright. "Remember the stories I told you about touring with The Turn Arounds?"

"I always forget that you did that."

"Trust me, *I* try to forget. But on that tour, I knew what to expect. The cheesy audiences reflected the cheesy music. But on this tour, it felt weird to play those songs to that crowd. We talked about it a lot. Especially midway through the tour, when our gratitude was starting to wear off."

"What do you mean?" I pinched my lower lip together with my fingers, trying to focus while also picturing

Rukmini and Kasi having long conversations. I wish I could have been there, that I had taken Rukmini up on her invitations to fly out for some of the shows.

"Rukmini felt like we were nobodies opening for this giant pop star."

"Even with all the attention around the cover?"

"Honestly, there were a lot of cities in Europe where no one had even heard of Rukmini. I don't think she felt she could be particularly critical of the situation though. And she didn't want to go back to being a freelance writer. But your tweet . . ."

"I should never have done that." I leaned forward to stand up but Kasi put her hand on my knee.

"No. You crystallized the problem. You set us free. I honestly feel relieved that it's all over."

"But it's not really over. Not for Rukmini," I said, pressing one of my bare feet over the other.

"You're right. It's not. And I don't know that she feels the same way I do."

"So, she's mad at me? Of course, she's mad at me."

"I don't know if mad is the right word." Now Kasi squirmed and glanced towards the door.

"Just say it," I pleaded.

"Well, I defended you. And that didn't go very well."

I pulled my head back. A part of me should have relished that I had been a cause for conflict but instead my guilt swelled up. "You did? Why did you do that?"

"I probably wouldn't have said what you said the way you said it. But you and I have history. And I also know how much Rukmini means to you. It's not like you would intentionally hurt her."

"So much history that you didn't think to tell me you were going on tour with her?" I would have been embarrassed to ask this question before, especially passive-aggressively, but my embarrassment bar had drastically lowered in the past months.

"It was meant to be a surprise!" Kasi smacked my knee excitedly.

"A surprise? Why?"

"Rukmini said that you were always talking about how you wanted to introduce us and that nothing would please you more than seeing your two close friends collaborating."

How had I managed to turn a surprise from a friend into a way to feel sorry for myself? Before I could figure out how to respond, Kasi continued, "Plus, you're the one who stopped responding to my texts."

"What are you talking about? The last text I got from you was a month before the tour." I plied out my phone from my jeans pocket and showed her the screen of her last text to me and mine to her, two unrelated questions, from two different years, locked in an incoherent conversation with each other. There was nothing more satisfying in a disagreement than proof.

Hey! I am just doing my taxes did
Marcus ever pay us for that
Turn Arounds gig from ages ago?

I will follow up. Thanks for the reminder.

How is Rukmini holding up?

"Wait, I never got that text from you! I haven't gotten any texts from you. That's why I finally decided to wait outside your house and stalk you," she said, holding up her phone to me and scrolling through a dozen texts that I never received.

"What the fuck?" we both said in unison.

"How is this possible?" I asked.

"I got a new phone right before the tour, but this is your number, right?" She showed my contact information to me.

"That's my number. Maybe you blocked me?" I said, half-kidding.

"No way! Why would I do that? This is some Mercury retrograde shit." She checked her settings. Had Rukmini gotten a new phone too somewhere on tour, or was there some other technical difficulty that would explain why I hadn't heard from her after she landed in Atlanta? As if she heard my thoughts, Kasi said, "Actually, I wonder if it has to do with all the international roaming?"

"Okay, Miss International."

"Neela!" She giggled. And then I did too. I couldn't remember the last time I had laughed in the company of a friend. The last time was probably with Rukmini. This thought made me cry while we continued laughing. Kasi was crying and laughing too. She probably hadn't laughed in a while either. Her last laughs had likely been shared with Rukmini too.

After our laughter subsided, I crossed over and sat beside her on the couch. I wanted to ask her more about Rukmini — *Where is she? Will she ever forgive me?* Instead I listened to her stories about the tour, riveted, sometimes even clapping. About how Hayley had asked for Kasi's permission to sample Indian music in her new songs. About how Rukmini had entertained her in their hotel rooms with impressions of Hayley's theatrical dancing. About the brown kids in the Houston audience who wore self-made T-shirts based on the 2001 Experimental Jetset merch, that read,

Rukmini&
Kasi&
Neela&
Malika

Hearing the last story, I placed my hand over my chest. Maybe Rukmini had been on to something when she had proposed we form a band, except maybe, in some alternate reality, the band was all four of us — as friends, as sisters. And in this perfect, musical haven, Malika was still alive.

Hearing Kasi's stories, her candidness, also made me think that maybe we were more than colleagues. Maybe my limited categorization had prevented us from growing closer all along.

"Let's do this again later this week?" I offered as she unlocked the front door.

"I would love that. Maybe call me to confirm instead of texting?" Kasi teased.

Before heading to bed, I turned on my computer to compose the new lines about respecting her that I had decided to add to my letter to Rukmini. My Twitter page was still open, and I had 89 notifications.

"Now what?" I sighed.

@neeladevaki pls sign this petition! @orionprize

Was this petition @neeladevaki's big announcement?

I just signed @neeladevaki's petition. If you care about fixing Canadian music you should too.

I pinched my eyelids together and then clicked the petition link included in these tweets.

We, the undersigned, are troubled by the recent inclusion of the ten-year-old album *Hegemony* by Subaltern Speaks on the Orion Prize shortlist.

According to the Orion Prize mandate, "eligible albums must be released in the previous year." Given the scarcity of cash music prizes in Canada, recognizing a ten-year-old album sets a dangerous precedent while also denying a spot on the list (and therefore potential prize money) to an artist who has produced an album within the stated timeline.

Beyond this, there have been questions raised about whether or not prize money should be potentially awarded to a band if one half — Malika Imani — is deceased, especially in light of complaints about misdirected profits that have been made by Imani's relatives.

There have also been looming concerns about the potentially racist promotion of this album, which is in direct opposition with the Canadian value of honouring diversity. This critique is especially significant given the recent conversations about racism in the music industry.

We hereby petition to have the nomination for Subaltern Speaks' *Hegemony* rescinded.

The petition had been signed 1,567 times in the last three hours. The signatories included Sumi and many of the famous musicians who had publicly congratulated Rukmini on her nomination.

I frantically typed @RUKMINI in the search field to see how she had responded.

Sorry, that page doesn't exist.

###

TOPS' EIGHT WITH RECLUSIVE MARCUS YOUNG

Lead singer of 2018 Orion Prize–winning band
The Turn Arounds
By Sumi Malhotra

1. Did you write a speech?

Our band is pretty easygoing, so no. Planning or practising ruins spontaneity. Plus, we assumed the award would go to an Indigenous or Black artist. Musicians like us aren't exactly popular these days.

2. Who were you rooting for this year?

Leonard Cohen. He's the best Canadian songwriter of all time and a huge inspiration for our band.

3. How did you celebrate?

I remember calling my dad, but everything else about that night is a blur. We all went to Fring's the day after.

4. What did you think of the controversy surrounding RUK-MINI and the Subaltern Speaks album *Hegemony*?

To be honest, I couldn't really keep up with it because I don't use social media — partly because of this cultural climate of political correctness. Everyone is trying to "out-woke" someone else, and music is supposed to be fun.

5. Have you listened to the album?

We listened to it a couple of times on the tour bus. It has that tribal-meets-political, M.I.A. kind of vibe. Very cool.

6. So do you disagree with the Orion jury's decision to rescind their nomination?

It was an unorthodox and maybe unfair choice to nominate an album that came out in 2007. But with all due respect to the Orion jury, I don't think it's right to give and then take away, or to cave to social justice warriors. Artists have a right to freedom of speech and expression.

7. You have played shows with Neela Devaki before. As a white man in a white-dominated industry, what did you think of her infamous subtweet, "Pandering to white people will get you everything"?

Neela is a beautiful human and we've had a great time with her in the past, so her tweet was a bit unexpected and maybe uncalled for. What's wrong with making music for everyone? Everyone's diversity is important. As a Caucasian, I am not of their descent, so obviously I can't speak to their experiences, but I'm not sure why these women can't seem to get along.

8. What's next for The Turn Arounds?

We are touring across Asia next year. We have never been out there, and we are stoked to keep building our global audience.

###

After Rukmini disappeared, I wanted to disappear too.

I couldn't be inside my apartment anymore. I couldn't be near a phone or a computer. So when I received Dr. Zuhur Imani's invitation to do an artist talk in her Word, Image, Sound class, I immediately said yes. Flying over Lake Michigan, I was reminded of the water whirling in my own body, that I was composed of actual matter and not just chemical reactions. A part of me wanted to dive out the plane window into the turquoise lake, if only to swim in the bigger picture.

It wasn't until I shook Dr. Imani's hand outside the stately university front doors that it occurred to me that coming here might have been another reckless decision. How would Rukmini feel about me meeting with Malika's cousin?

"It's lovely to meet you, Neela. I am a long-time admirer," Dr. Imani said, adjusting her thick maroon glasses.

"It's nice to meet you too, Dr. Imani. This is my first time in Minnesota."

"Please, call me Zuhur. And thanks for coming down to the sacred birthplace of Prince." Zuhur smiled at the sky, as if to greet the icon's ghost, holding the door open for me and putting me at ease. Inside, the building seemed more like a church than a school, with the smell of ancient wood and gothic stained-glass windows. Was this a deliberate effort to instill reverence, or even fear, in students?

"I forgot that this was his hometown. Do you teach his work in your class?"

"Of course. I think Prince is mandatory course content for any arts-related class in Minneapolis."

"I should have studied in Minneapolis. I could be one of your students." I had never felt a pull towards academia, but was this because I had never imagined the possibility of a brown woman professor?

"You wouldn't want a groupie as a teacher," Zuhur joked and pointed at a poster in the hallway stapled on top of other colourful posters. It featured an awkward crop of my press photo, information about the event and a title in block letters: *NEELA DEVAKI: HER* SELF & *HER MUSIC*.

The lecture hall was larger than I expected, an upside-down pyramid of maroon seats. "How many students do you have?"

"This is an intro course so there's a good hundred or so. As I mentioned in the email, we spent last week listening to *Selfhood* and then discussing modalities of autonomy by women of colour in art, so anything you want to add on that, or anything else, would be perfect." Zuhur wrote my name, website and handle in loopy cursive on the whiteboard.

After the students filled the seats, Zuhur tugged the bottom of her grey blazer and said, "We are very fortunate to have the artist who created the album we have been studying as our guest today. The singular Neela Devaki."

The students applauded respectfully.

"Please put your phones away and give our guest the attention she deserves."

Zuhur joined the rest of her students in the seats and I lay down on the carpet below the whiteboard. I breathed deliberately and after I stopped noticing the smell of a laundry hamper, I turned my head towards the class. "This is how *Selfhood* began. For me to rediscover my independence, I had to slow down and tune in to my body again."

Then I moved into the first song from the album. Not accustomed to performing in classrooms, the flicking of the florescent lights browbeat me into closing my eyes. Inevitably, my mind wandered to Rukmini and her debut class performance. I'd pictured her in a smaller, high school–style classroom, but with this many students I could see why she'd be nervous. Then I thought of Malika, how strange it was that now, all these years later, I was on the floor of her cousin's classroom, singing for her students.

When I finished singing, I stood up and the class applauded vigorously, as though they were trying to make up for their timid welcome.

Zuhur joined me at the front of the room. "Thank you for your incredible performance. I'm sure we all agree that the experience of hearing you live has deepened our connection to the album." Many of the students clapped again. Others fervently typed on their laptops. What were they writing?

"Why don't I start the Q&A?" Zuhur offered. "Did you make *Selfhood* as an act of resistance towards the resurgence of girl groups of colour?"

Was this a pointed question? Was she referring to Subaltern Speaks? Was this why she had invited me?

"Truthfully, I haven't noticed a resurgence," I responded, stepping slightly away from Zuhur and addressing the students instead. "*Selfhood* is more of an act of resistance towards the emphasis of coupledom in pop music broadly."

I waited for Zuhur's rebuttal, but when a student in overalls and violet lipstick in the front row raised her hand, I gestured in her direction.

"Hi, I'm Samira. Thank you, Neela, for making *Selfhood*. So refreshing to hear what a woman might sing if she isn't singing about a man or a romantic relationship! It felt a bit like a musical equivalent of the Bechdel movie test. So are the mostly wordless songs meant to echo how the voices of single women are culturally inaudible?"

"Thank you for the compliment, Samira." I advanced closer to Samira and continued, "To answer your question, I agree that single women are often ignored, or the opposite, we're scrutinized, because we're seen as failures." In my peripheral vision, I could see Zuhur nodding. "But the choice to move away from language wasn't specifically tied to making a huge statement. I just spend a lot of time alone in my apartment and my favourite moments are the rare ones that are word-free, thought-free . . . tweet-free."

Many of the students nodded, and some giggled at their laptop screens. From there, the Q&A devolved into the white students asking me questions pertaining to their own art projects and ambitions.

"We have time for one last question," Zuhur declared after checking a rusty wall clock behind her.

Samira's hand shot up, the multicoloured bangles around her wrist jingling. After Zuhur scanned for other students with questions, she said "Go ahead and ask your question, Samira."

"Um, well, I wanted to ask you about your recent subtweet." Samira paused and looked at Zuhur who then looked at me with her hands open, wordlessly asking, "Are you comfortable with answering this?" I nodded at both of them. *Of course* students would be interested in social media drama. The group of students in the back row who had been zipping up their backpacks stopped rustling.

"Okay. Do you think, in a white supremacist society, it's even possible to create art that doesn't on some level pander to white people? And where are the lines between owning your own culture in your art versus pandering if white people are often the main consumers?"

I exhaled and the sound seemed to reverberate in the hush of the room. This wasn't the accusatory or commendatory question I had anticipated. "I want to say that it comes down to intention. Are you wearing your bindi in your photo or rhyming with 'curry' in your rap as a way to revel in your culture? Or are you trying get white people to like you, the flattened idea of you they have because of your skin colour?"

Samira frowned and put up her hand again, and without waiting for me to motion to her, she spoke faster. "But isn't it unfair to criticize artists of colour for wanting to appeal to white people when they've ingrained in us to value their approval the most? Plus their approval usually means access to resources. Wasn't your criticism ultimately misdirected?"

I knew that I had been unfair to Rukmini, but I had been too close to the chaos to make the links that Samira articulated. Why did Rukmini warrant more public criticism than Bart or Hayley or even Marcus for the roles they play in upholding this lopsided system? Stupefied, I stumbled backwards. "Uh . . ."

Before I could respond further, Zuhur interjected, "Those are great questions, Samira. Why don't we circle back to them at the start of next class. And don't forget that your assignments are also due next week."

"I should have prepared better for the last question," I admitted as we trekked through the crisscrossing hallways to the campus pub, where Zuhur had offered to take me for dinner.

"I don't think there is an easy answer when interrogating the slipperiness of brown cultural production in white . . . hegemonies." Zuhur paused. "What you said about intention was perfect. So was your performance. Malika would have loved it."

I had anticipated that Malika would come up in conversation with Zuhur at some point. I wanted to learn more about her music, about what had happened in the span of time between her university graduation and her death, to collect the pieces of Malika's story that Rukmini had been missing.

"That's nice to hear."

"Yeah, I think she would have really liked you." Zuhur passed me her phone, a photo open onscreen.

"Is this her?"

It was a studio portrait of Malika in her graduation hat and gown in front of a standard royal-blue backdrop. I remembered how much I wanted to know what Malika looked like when *Hegemony* had surfaced, but now I wished I hadn't found out. Seeing this photograph made the puzzle clearer: Rukmini had likely had her own portrait taken right before or right after Malika. They had likely cheered each other on, fixed each other's hair and checked each other's teeth to make sure they were free of any food they might have eaten together before. This photo captured a time when they were friends, unaware that days later they no longer would be.

"Yes. She was like my little sister."

"You do look alike."

"Minus the grey hair." Zuhur shook her head to draw my attention to her white strands.

"We actually sounded alike too," she continued after we found a half-moon booth in the back of the pub. "We loved calling each other's parents and pretending we were each other. They could never tell us apart."

"Cheeky."

We both looked down at our menus, not knowing what to say next. We sunk into the sounds of the hockey game shouting on the TVs around us and the smell of bubbling fryer oil.

"I wish she would at least reach out to me." Zuhur sighed, still pretending to read her menu.

"Who?" I asked, pretending not to know that she meant Rukmini.

"Rukmini." She finally looked up but gazed in the direction of the bar, searching the room for a server.

"Did you try to contact her?" Hearing my words aloud, the question sounded defensive, but I meant it sincerely.

"No. Why would I? I'm sure she knew I existed. She definitely knows now. She could easily find me online." Now it was my turn to look for a server. When I turned back, Zuhur and I looked at each other, both knowing we could no longer avoid this conversation. And maybe it was one she needed to have. Maybe I needed it too.

"Can I ask what you would want Rukmini to say?"

Zuhur sat upright. "I've actually thought about this a lot."

"And?"

"For the longest time, I wanted an apology. But when I thought about it more, I wasn't sure what I wanted her to apologize for. For performing songs that are half hers? Or for not pursuing music with Mali? I saw the toll Mali's music career took on her, and I wouldn't wish that on anyone. And ask me if I am still close with my university friends. Life happens." She pushed her menu aside as though she was no longer hungry.

"Life happens," she repeated and laughed wryly. "Unless you die. And when Malika died, everyone around me said, 'Sorry for your loss.' And I hated the way the words *your loss* cleanly glossed over a name and a human life. Over Malika's life. But it also suggested that *I* was the only one who had lost someone. Malika's death was a loss for everyone. Not just me." Zuhur banged her fist on the table. "In the end, that was the acknowledgement that I wanted from Rukmini. I wanted to hear her say, 'Sorry for *our* loss. Sorry Malika didn't have more time.'"

I reached my hand across the table and she squeezed it. We sat together with our heads bowed, our tears dripping around our mouths. I wanted to tell Zuhur about Rukmini's extensive search for Malika, and that I was sure Rukmini was devastated when she found out about Malika's death, but I worried it would sound like I was defending her.

Instead I offered, "Well, if it's okay for me to say, I am sorry that I never got a chance to meet Malika. Her production on the album was ahead of its time, which is being proven now."

"Actually," Zuhur said, letting go of my hand to wipe her eyes with her serviette, "when I came across your music years ago, I sent it to Malika and suggested she message you about collaborating somehow."

"You did? What was her response?"

"I honestly can't remember. At some point, music became too sensitive of a topic to broach. Especially when she took a cashier job at a grocery store."

"I get it. Believe me."

"Do you think I could send you some of her solo work sometime?"

"I would be honoured."

Zuhur reached back for my still stretched hand. This bridge wouldn't bring Malika back but perhaps it could stand for the memorial she was long due.

###

On my flight back to Toronto, I couldn't stop thinking about whether or not Malika had messaged me. Had I responded? Thinking about her name in my inbox also reminded me of my computer, the petition, everything. But seeing the pools of water through the window again, I remembered the feeling I had on the flight to Minneapolis. I knew I had to find a way to extend the short break from my home life that visiting Zuhur's class had given me. This meant quitting my transcription job and looking for a different way to pay my bills.

I had noticed a *Help Wanted* sign at Grapefruit Moon the Saturday I had spent there waiting for Rukmini. Although I had no formal experience as a server, when I went in to apply, the manager hired me on the spot. It turned out the server who had waited on me that Saturday was also the manager.

"This isn't a sympathy hire, right?" I asked.

"No one feels sorry for you, Neela," he responded. I wasn't not sure what he meant, if he was referring to the subtweet or the petition. I also didn't care. If anything, I was relieved to hear that I wasn't the object of pity.

I didn't mind standing for hours, and strangely I didn't mind having to talk pleasantly to customer after customer. I even attempted Rukmini's Female Tone Trinity. The work was exhausting, but it was the kind of exhaustion that I needed: the kind that prevented me from going online, the kind that forced me to crash on my bed every night after work, the kind that gifted me with sleep. Being a server had obliterated my insomnia, and I was grateful for uninterrupted hours of darkness. I became so addicted that I requested additional shifts.

The best part of the job was that when a customer complained about their bacon not being crispy enough, or the onions in the macaroni, or the lack of organic options, the complaints were never a comment on my or anyone else's character. I'm sure some of my customers disliked the food, how long they had to wait for it or even my demeanor. But in the restaurant, I never had to question whether I was a bad or a good person. I wasn't a role model and I wasn't a bitch.

Of course, I thought about Rukmini every day.

"You are taking a job at the café you two used to hang out at together?" Since our reunion, and especially during the Orion debacle, Kasi and I had been meeting frequently by my place at Greenwood Park. One of the only drawbacks of this job was that I was now seeing her less often than I wanted.

"Yes." I nodded, holding the chains of the swing on either side of me and smearing the sand with my feet.

"That's an interesting way to punish yourself," Kasi noted and then kicked her swing upward.

"It's not really about punishment."

"Sure it is," Kasi yelled from above me. I joined her and for ten minutes, as the sky dimmed to pink, our swings were synchronized.

When we both slowed down, she added, "I really think she will . . . reach out in time . . . you'll see." We stumbled on the sand and past the empty outdoor pool towards my place. I was already looking forward to morning laps with Kasi when it reopened next summer.

"And if she doesn't?" I asked.

"And if she doesn't?" Kasi repeated, swinging her arm around my shoulder.

And if she didn't reach out, I knew that one day Rukmini would be unable to resist the lure of her favourite café. I wasn't delusional enough to believe we would be friends again, but someday I would apologize in person.

After a month as a server, I started getting calls from an unknown number. I refused to answer. The last time I made that mistake, I ended up having to talk to Bart Gold. The caller continued to phone for three days in a row, and eventually hope implored me to pick up.

"Rukmini?" I stammered, as I locked myself in the staff washroom.

"Hi Neela, this is Hayley Trace!" The voice sounded like a teenager at her sweet sixteen birthday party.

"Oh. Hi." I should have said, "Bye."

"I hope you don't mind me calling. Bart gave me your number."

"I'm just on a coffee break at work. Is there something I can help you with?" I put her on speaker phone and held the phone away from me, tempted to drop it into the toilet.

"I sure hope so," she squeaked. "Do you have time to meet tomorrow?"

"What is this about?"

"It will be *so* much easier to explain in person."

"Fine. Why don't you come by my work? My shift ends at 4 p.m." If we had to meet, I knew I would feel better if it was around my work hours, like a job.

"Perfect. Text me the address? Looking forward to meeting you. Ciao!"

What did Hayley Trace want from me?

Throughout my shift the next day, especially during the brief solitary moments of wiping the tables after my customers left, I tried to guess. Had Rukmini asked Hayley to deliver a message to me? Perhaps a response to my letter? Or was Hayley going to inform me that Rukmini had some kind of illness or was leaving the country?

The previous night, I had debated whether or not to text her the address. I convinced myself that she would bail once she Google Mapped the location and decided she was too famous to come to a small neighbourhood café. But as soon as I texted her, she followed me on Twitter and Instagram and liked all of my recent photos. I started to regret suggesting we meet at Grapefruit Moon. Picturing her there felt like an intrusion, a corruption.

Hayley Trace arrived at the restaurant at exactly 4 p.m., wearing a white slip dress that looked like a doily, with no jacket, even though it was autumn. Never enough attention.

"Neela Devaki, at last," she declared and leaned in to embrace me.

I leaned away and said, "Why don't we sit at the back." Though it probably seemed like I was being respectful of her privacy, especially since customers had definitely noticed her when she had walked in (as she had intended) and reached for their phones, I mostly didn't want her anywhere near the table I had once shared regularly with Rukmini. I also worried that on the slight chance that Rukmini finally decided to come in today, she would see me and Hayley together and assume we were now friends or, worse, that we were conspiring against her.

"This a cozy place," Hayley observed, pressing her lips together a few times as she checked her lipstick in one of the large mirrors hanging on the white brick wall next to our table. I had always thought mirrors were eccentric choices for décor. Who wanted to watch themselves eat? Now I had my answer.

"It's hard to imagine you working here."

"Why, because it's not some fine dining bistro?"

"No, because you are a rock star," she said with what sounded like reverence and flipped her phone onto its front side to show me how focused she was. "I just assumed that you wouldn't need to be working a day job after *Selfhood*."

"You've listened to *Selfhood*?"

"Of course! Marcus and I have it on repeat when we go to the gym."

"You and Marcus know each other?

"We're dating," she gushed. "We met backstage at the Orion Awards." I tried not to roll my eyes. Of course they did. I could easily picture them together in matching white doily attire, his fashioned into an Asian-inspired tunic, having high tea at the King Eddy or taking her poodle into posh Yorkville boutiques.

"Well, *Selfhood* is not exactly workout music." Hayley Trace was a liar. Hayley Trace had definitely not listened to my album.

"I prefer not to listen to dance music when I work out. I find hard beats kind of distracting. Your music grounds me. Keeps me focused."

Wow, she was good. I could understand why Rukmini and Kasi had stayed on tour with her for as long as they did. But I wasn't them.

"I suppose you need to remain focused when you are planning who you are going to use next?"

Hayley drew her head back. "*Use?* What do you mean?"

"You know what I mean. What you did to Rukmini."

"I think you have me all wrong. I never set out to use Rukmini. Never." The sweetness in her voice started to fade. This shift only encouraged me. Come out and play, Hayley. Let's have this out, one bitch to another.

I crossed my arms. "Is that what you tell yourself?"

"You don't understand. I was . . . am a big Rukmini and Malika fan. That's why I did it."

"That's why you booted Rukmini off your tour? That doesn't make any fucking sense."

Hayley didn't respond right away. She widened her shoulders and scanned my face. Did she expect that I would just fawn? I took a breath and surveyed the restaurant, starting to fill up for the happy hour rush. Even though I was off the clock, I couldn't afford to be seen yelling at a pretty white famous woman in my workplace.

"Wait. Did you know Malika?"

Hayley looked away and then nodded.

"How? When?"

"In university," she whispered and glanced behind her. My co-worker who was rolling forks and knifes into napkins at the bar counter met her eye and waved sheepishly.

"You knew Malika in university? You studied in Toronto?"

"I was born here. I just don't advertise that because it's kind of the kiss of death in the music industry," she said, still in a hushed tone. Did she think I was wearing a wire?

"So, were you friends?"

"Classmates. Rukmini's classmate too."

"She never mentioned you."

"She didn't remember me. I was just another brown haired, big-rimmed-glasses-wearing white girl with a passion for feminist theory. We kind of all look the same." I wanted to laugh but she laughed first and formed two circles with her fingers over her eyes, trying to show me her nerdy past. "I also wasn't 'Hayley Trace' then."

"Who were you?"

"Stacilyn. Stacilyn Hallestein."

I snorted. "Stacilyn Hallestein? Are you fucking kidding me?"

"See? You would've changed your name too."

"It's not that bad," I said, momentarily feeling guilty. Then it hit me. "Holy shit. You saw the Subaltern Speaks presentation."

"I did!" she exclaimed as though she had been waiting for me to guess. The couple sitting at the table behind Hayley turned their heads in our direction.

"What was it like?

"Incredible. Think of everything that has been said about *Hegemony* and multiply it by ten. I was there, right in the front row. Hollywood agents talk about . . ."

I rolled my eyes.

"Hollywood agents," she repeated and tossed her hair, "talk about the moment they see a star come to life. That's how I felt watching Rukmini and Malika. I was haunted by their performance for years after we graduated. Their rare combination of innocence and power. They inspired me to move to L.A. and make music myself."

"How novel. Another white pop star's career built from the inspiration of artists of colour."

"Exactly," she said eagerly, with no defensiveness in her tone. "That's why I did it," she said again, leaning closer. Her breath smelled like watermelon gum.

"Did what?"

"That's why I leaked the album."

"What? No. It was a random . . ." My mouth hung open.

"A random classmate? That was me. I set up a fake Twitter account. Took half a second," she bragged.

"Why would you do that?"

"Oh, you know. My white guilt. There I was, my music career skyrocketing, but I still couldn't stop thinking about Subaltern Speaks. How much they deserved what was basically being handed to me." She paused politely, waiting for me to take another jab but also confident she had beaten me to it. My mind pinged between all the content I'd absorbed since *Hegemony* had leaked, trying to compile an accurate history.

"Not that I didn't work hard out there," she continued, pulling a loose strand of hair off her shoulder and rolling it into a ball with her thumb and finger. "But it's not the same for me as it is for you, right? Anyways, when I heard Rukmini's cover of your song, I didn't recognize her name, but I recognized that voice. That voice that I had been listening to for a decade."

"So, you leaked their album . . ."

"I did. It felt necessary. Like my small way of creating balance. Equality."

"Oh, you think that's all it takes?"

"No, of course not." She chuckled and now rolled her eyes at me. "That's why I also anonymously sent the album to all the digital outlets and my press contacts. That's why I had Bart reach out to invite her to open for me."

"Why didn't you just share the link to the album from your own account? Why all the secrecy?"

"You know, I thought about doing that." She leaned her hand on her fist, pondering her choice. "But I thought that would look too 'white saviour-y,'" she said, using air quotes. Startled that a white person could easily expunge any criticism with four bunny ears folding up and down, I pulled back but was careful not to lean too hard, remembering the stairs descending behind me. I should have sat on the other side.

"Why are you telling me all of this? Does Rukmini know?"

"I never told her. I actually kept my distance from her on the tour so that she wouldn't recognize me face to face. And I'm telling you because I thought you might want to know? It also feels really good to tell someone. Someone close to all the players." Then she shrugged and said, "Or maybe I want you to see that I'm not a bad person," making direct eye contact with me. For a moment, she almost seemed sincere.

"So, this is why you asked to meet? To unburden and absolve yourself?"

"Oh no, not at all. I didn't actually plan on telling you any of this."

"Aren't you worried that I'll share this information?"

"Not really. I think you've probably learned your lesson about sharing too much," she said and checked the time on her phone. "Besides, you were the one who subtweeted me about wanting the real tea at Grapefruit Moon."

"Do you think everything on the internet is about you?" I hissed.

"Hey, sorry to interrupt, but can we get a selfie?" asked the young woman from the couple behind Hayley.

"Of course!" Hayley said. She took the woman's phone and held her arm in the air. "Actually, my good friend Neela will take it for us." She handed me the phone. I considered telling all three of them to fuck off, but I was still at my workplace.

"Everyone say, 'Hey! Hey! Hayley!'" she ordered, which they did in unison, along with some of the other patrons in the café who were making peace signs, trying to photobomb.

How many times had Hayley put her "good friends" Rukmini and Kasi to work like this? After I returned the woman's phone, I put my hands on the table and prepared to stand up.

"Okay, what did you want to tell me?"

Hayley Trace put her hands on top of mine and said, "I'm having a show in Toronto in a few months and I'm hoping you'll open for me."

###

*T*he last thing Sumi wanted to do was go to a Neela Devaki show.

She was tired of seeing, and of typing, her name. Not just hers. Rukmini's name too. And Hayley's name. Maybe even her own name.

You are going to cover this, right?

That was the message her editor sent her with a link announcing Hayley's show in a month.

Sumi responded, I think this story is officially overplayed.

Are you kidding? Neela Devaki and Hayley Trace at the SkyDome? Together? This has clicks and Sumi Malhotra written all over it!

After years of carefully curating a portfolio of cerebral reviews of underrated bands, her writing was finally being consumed — widely. With that one article about Rukmini, she had become not just a respected music critic but a popular one. But these recent stories were not what she wanted to be known for.

Later that night, as two skinny white boys with long hair and nose piercings banged on their bass and drums respectively, Bart Gold yelled into her ear, "Sumi, I gotta tell you, you inspired this new direction for me." The lead singer screamed into a mic plugged into a distortion pedal and pumped his fist in the air as though he and his band had invented sound. She wondered how many private music lessons these boys had received and how much of the gear onstage had been paid for by their parents, who were probably at their cottages at this moment, reading back issues of *Toronto Life*.

"Do I have you to blame for this déjà vu?" she barked back at Bart, ignoring his compliment and tilting her head at the stage. When Sumi had received his invitation to meet at the Drake, she had assumed that he would try to charm her into profiling one of his hot new artists. She said yes to the meeting because she wanted the chance to contradict what Rukmini had once said — to prove that it was, in fact, possible to say no to Bart Gold.

He winked at her. She almost gagged but, eager to move the night along, she asked, "So, what's this new direction?" She now suspected that he was going to ask her to assist him with diversifying his artist roster. She swallowed the last of her scotch, preparing to deliver an emphatic *NO*.

"Gold & Platinum is dipping into rubbishing!" Despite the low lighting in the bar, his yellow stained teeth glowed. Suddenly she craved a smoke.

"NO," she declared, as planned. The straight couple in front of them, who had been making out throughout the show and during the breaks, turned around and glared at her. She glared back and forcefully puckered the air, imitating them. Then she backtracked, "Wait, what the fuck is rubbishing?"

"Publishing!" Bart yelled, enunciating more carefully this time. "The interest in your stories has confirmed that there's a healthy market for incisive music writing. Bloomsbury was ahead of this trend with their 33 1/3 series."

Sumi recoiled from the mention of 33 1/3. Years ago, she had pitched a proposal for a book about Tinashe's debut mixtape, but it hadn't even made it past the first round of cuts. She pushed her index finger over the ear he had shouted in. "So what does this have to do with me?" She lifted her bomber jacket hanging over her arm and put it on.

"We haven't figured out the details," Bart explained, following her out of the venue.

Once they had escaped into the less noisy hallway and were moving up the staircase to the main floor, he continued at a regular volume, "But we are thinking of publishing a collection of two to three boundary defying music-related books a year for the discerning reader. We would love for you to be the editor."

"Fuck," Sumi blurted and stopped on the steps. She hadn't expected Bart Gold to offer her the Dream Job.

"Did you forget something in the bar? Your purse?"

"Bart, I don't own a purse."

"Well, agree to be our editor and I can help you with that." He winked again. "And if you don't like that idea, I have a backup plan."

She felt obligated to smile but resumed climbing. "I bet you do."

Bart slumped down on the distressed leather sofa in the back of the lobby and patted the cushion beside him, summoning Sumi. She stayed standing.

"Well, maybe you see yourself as more of a writer than an editor?" he continued. "If that's the case, we can explore that path instead. I could imagine you writing a book on Subaltern Speaks or even on Neela Devaki? Or both? It could include some of the articles you have already written if we can get the rights from *Toronto Tops*?"

"Fuck," she repeated a week later, still weighing her options. She had hoped she would have made a decision by now, so she could quit her job and skip the concert. But quitting would mean saying yes to Bart Gold (though she would definitely say no to writing a book about any of those women). And saying yes to Bart would make her a fucking hypocrite.

So for now she focused on the task at hand, opening up Twitter on her unscratched gunmetal laptop. She knew the key aspect of the story she had to uncover was motive. Why would Neela do a joint show with Hayley Trace after basically condemning Rukmini for opening for Hayley? As part of her preparation for writing this piece, she examined the responses to the announcement online, trying not to respond.

Just scored tickets for @NeelaDevaki's comeback
show! #NeelaStan

(Hey kid, Neela never retired?)

Maybe @NeelaDevaki will bring @RUKMINI onstage
for some kind of reunion? Maybe that's why she is
doing this?

(Doubtful. This isn't fucking Lilith Fair.)

There were also dozens of critical tweets and hashtags.

#fromSelfhoodtoSellout
#rukminisreplacement
#fuckinghypocrite

Predictable. Eventually Sumi tweeted from her own
account,

What if it's just good money? #capitalism

Following her piece on Rukmini, Sumi had received a
text from her, after months of infrequent communication,
containing that single word: Why?

What an entitled, and even offensive, question to ask.
"Why" suggested that there had to be a reason beyond the
reason provided in the article, an ulterior motive, a more
logical explanation.

But there was no logic beyond truth. In her piece
about Rukmini, she had simply reported the facts. She
was a journalist after all (at least for now), and she took

her job seriously. She had said what needed to be said —
and the proof was in the response.

What interested her more was that Hayley's name
seemed to have disappeared from the discussions on
the upcoming show. The focus of this event was Neela
Devaki. Hayley must have noticed this too because one
week before the show, Sumi received a press release from
Gold & Platinum Entertainment.

GLOBAL POPSTAR HAYLEY TRACE LAUNCHES M.I.C. INITIATIVE

New Malika Imani Camp for Girls of Colour

"No fucking way," Sumi said aloud and continued to
skim the rest of the press release.

> "I was absolutely devastated reading the news
> about Malika Imani's untimely death. I am a huge
> fan of her Subaltern Speaks project and I couldn't
> stop thinking about all the music inside of her that
> we never got to hear. Because of systemic barriers
> in the music industry, I am told by my women of
> colour musician friends that they experience their
> own forms of silence and erasure. So in honour of
> Malika's life and visionary music, and inspired by
> Girls Rock Camp, I'm launching M.I.C. — the Malika
> Imani Camp for girls of colour, where young female

musicians of colour can be empowered and be offered mentorship and skill-building from industry experts." — Hayley Trace

To support M.I.C., visit hayleymicproject.com or download/stream the new single "Calling In" now available on all platforms. All proceeds from the single will be going to M.I.C. development and programming.

"Oh, this is going to be good." Sumi rapidly clicked on the link to listen to the single. Unlike Hayley's previous hits, this one featured no beats or synths. Instead it was just her voice backed by a grand piano, string section and a gospel choir. Sumi grabbed a pen and scribbled down the opening lyrics on her notepad.

We were so hard on you (so hard)
We made a fool of you (so cruel)
You might have made some mistakes
But we are just as much to blame

We should have called you in (not out)
We should have given you the benefit of the doubt
We should have called you up not out online
If we could do it all again and go back in time
We would call, call, call, call you in.

Sumi cackled. "D2, you have to come hear this shit. It's priceless," she said, tearing out her earbuds and spinning around to see the deserted cubicle desk behind her.

No one else seemed to find Hayley's desperate PR stunt as amusing and obnoxious as Sumi. Instead, Hayley's initiative was unanimously praised. The single raised speculation about it being an apology song to Rukmini and spawned new think-pieces in defence of Rukmini, extolling Hayley for pointing out the broader societal complicity in what had transpired. And all of this activity successfully drowned out mentions of Neela.

Yet on the eve of the show, as Sumi walked into the SkyDome, she spotted teenagers carrying #TeamNeela signs and sporting versions of Neela's short shaggy crop. She also noticed how few empty seats there were inside the stadium for an opener. One year ago, Neela Devaki could have barely filled a three-hundred capacity room.

When the background music stopped, all of the house lights came on. The audience lifted their phones. A small figure in a silver dress materialized, walked past the centre mic and stood at the edge of the stage. The crowd screamed. Sumi didn't need to look at the oversized monitor above the stage to recognize the woman.

"Hi Neela," Sumi said aloud.

She recalled the day she had found Neela's self-titled debut album in the sale bin at HMV nine years ago. She'd been startled by seeing a brown woman on an album cover, let alone a brown woman who appeared to be so close to her age. Taking the CD to the listening booth, she had balanced on the blue stool and absorbed the album in its entirety. At first, hearing Neela's bassy tone had felt hollowing, like a kind of death. Sumi felt herself unravelling. But the longer she listened, the more she felt as though Neela's voice was refilling every crevice in her body. This had to be what love sounded like. She bought the album and, although she loathed the word *fan*, she bought every album that Neela put out on the day of its release.

When she had started her job at *Toronto Tops*, her first pitch had been a feature on Neela.

"Never heard of her," her editor scoffed.

"That's the point of a feature," she replied.

"We aren't in the business of featuring nobodies."

Sumi's memories were interrupted by a second wave of cheering. Another woman had walked on stage.

"Rukmini?" she whispered — along with others in the crowd.

Sumi could feel her throat start to close up. She remembered how Rukmini had abandoned her at The Turn Arounds' show the first time she had seen Neela perform. Rukmini hadn't texted Sumi to apologize until the following day, and then she had called her to gush about Neela as though she had discovered her.

"Do you know who she is?" Rukmini had asked Sumi audaciously. "I kind of want to ask her out for coffee or something."

"You should." Sumi had encouraged her partly

because they were friends, and she wanted to seem supportive. Realistically, she couldn't imagine rock star Neela Devaki saying yes. If she had imagined that was a possibility, she would have asked Neela out herself, instead of working for years to create a more professional way to establish a connection.

But Neela did say yes to Rukmini. And then Neela and Rukmini became friends, went to shows, talked about music. When Sumi ran into the two of them together at the AGO, she wasn't sure which of them she envied more. But Rukmini's cover of Neela's song, draining it of its artistry and monopolizing the acclaim, was not a grey area to Sumi.

When the woman onstage sat down at the piano behind Neela, Sumi realized her mistake. It was Kasi. While Neela continued to look out at the crowd in silence, Sumi wondered how she felt now, being watched by thousands. Was she missing the intimacy of the smaller clubs she typically played? Or was this her way of seeing what Rukmini had seen every night before Hayley had thrown her off the tour? Because she had seen Neela perform live several times before, she knew that this silent prolonged gaze was a standard part of Neela's show, but tonight she wasn't just looking at the audience — she was searching. Was she hoping to see Rukmini?

Following Neela's lead, Sumi scanned the faces around her. She paused when she spotted a grey-haired brown woman sporting a striped collared shirt and maroon glasses. She looked like she had come directly from work. Why did this woman look so familiar? Had she sat next to her on the subway? Or was she the relative of a friend? Or someone connected to *Toronto Tops*?

These questions made Sumi's hand instinctively wave at the woman. Then she recognized her from her profile on the university website — Dr. Imani. Of course, she had flown in for this show. Of course, she was a Neela fan too.

Embarrassed that Dr. Imani likely didn't know what Sumi looked like since their interview had been conducted by phone, she quickly turned around, just in time to see Neela walk to the mic and nod at Kasi. Sumi watched them smile at each other in the monitors. Then Neela's voice, in all its grandeur, filled the arena.

Nobody can see my isolation
Nobody can see how much I want to be friends

It took a moment for the crowd, and for Sumi, to recognize the song. When they did, there was a collective gasp.

"Which theorist wrote the lyrics of the last song?" Sumi had asked Rukmini when she had seen her in the office the week after the Subaltern Speaks album had leaked.

"'Wanting'? Malika wrote them," Rukmini said quietly. "She figured we could use a break from the class material. We put it on *Hegemony* as a bonus track."

"It's the best song on the album," Sumi declared.

"You're just saying that." Rukmini rolled her chair into Sumi's.

"Have you ever known me to just say anything?"

"You're just trying to cheer me up because of what I told you about my falling-out with Malika."

"Nope. It's a rare and genuine compliment. Just accept it, D2," Sumi said, spinning Rukmini's chair around.

Nobody can see my wanting
Don't want to be wanting

As Sumi listened to Neela covering this Subaltern Speaks song, she thought about Malika. She pictured all the arenas Malika's songs had been performed in and the crowds they had been played to — arenas Malika would never see, and applause she would never hear.

She thought about Rukmini too, about seeing her close her Detroit set with this same song. Although Sumi's confidence in the validity of her criticisms was unwavering, she had never intended to silence Rukmini.

Because wanting is dangerous
Wanting is dangerous

She wished Rukmini could see and hear this tribute. How Neela delivered every word and note with careful precision, cutting through layer after layer of human tissue. How still and grateful the stadium was, as though the audience had waited eons to be sliced open and have their hearts revealed. Maybe Rukmini's heart would feel restored. Maybe she would reemerge.

I'll suppress the beast, I'll be my best for now

As Neela's final notes crescendoed, the live video in the monitor cut to a still image — two open mouths laughing. Rukmini's and Malika's mouths. The *Hegemony* artwork.

The crowd released their screams at last. After the song ended, Neela stepped to the front of the stage again and bowed majestically.

"*Neela! Neela!*" the crowd chanted. Sumi thought she could also hear some people yelling, "*Rukmini! Rukmini!*"

Then Neela and Kasi exited the stage, hand in hand. The screen cut to black.

The audience's cheers turned into another collective gasp and then into boos when it became clear that Neela and Kasi weren't returning.

Sumi thought about brown women who become ghosts.

Then her body rose on its own, hands applauding, and her legs carried her out of the stadium.

###

REFERENCES

Fanon, Frantz. *Black Skin, White Masks*. Translated by
Richard Filcox. New York: Grove, 1952.

Jordan, June. "A New Politics of Sexuality." In *Technical
Difficulties*, 187–193. New York: Pantheon, 1992.

Kameir, Rawiya (@rawiya). "listen it's ok to not write
a book." Twitter. January 30, 2018. https://twitter.
com/rawiya/status/958369607852716032.

Lorde, Audre. "The Transformation of Silence into
Language and Action." *Sister Outsider*. New York:
Publisher Crossing Press/Penguin Random House,
1984, 2007.

McLeod, Melvin. "'There's No Place to Go but Up': bell hooks and Maya Angelou in Conversation." *Lion's Roar*. January 1, 1998.

Munday, Evan (@idontlikemunday). "You're so vain, I bet you think this novel's about you." Twitter. August 13, 2019. https://twitter.com/idontlikemunday/status/1161309900011638784.

Roy, Arundhati, and Avni Sejpal. "How to Think About Empire." *Boston Review*. January 3, 2019.

Spivak, Gayatri Chakravorty. "Can the Subaltern Speak?" In *Marxism and the Interpretation of Culture*, edited by Cary Nelson and Lawrence Grossberg, 24–28. London: Macmillan, 1988.

ACKNOWLEDGEMENTS

In a story that is in many ways about ideas and ownership, it is imperative for me to honour and credit the many unseen hours of idea generating that friends and peers have invested in this book — in the form of generous and challenging feedback in Word documents and Google Docs, late-night brainstorming sessions on the phone about defying tropes, meals spent reconstructing plot lines and countless text exchanges encouraging me to just keep writing.

More succinctly, this book would not exist without the ideas generated by and gifted to me from Adam Holman, Trisha Yeo, Shemeena Shraya and Amber Dawn — or without your immeasurable care. Thank you for loving me (and these characters), for standing by my side and for reminding me to stand by my vision.

Nor would this book exist without Jen Knoch and ECW Press. Thank you for being a believer.

Thank you Crissy Calhoun (and Jen, again) for giving me the space to write the book I had to write and your thoughtful edits. Isn't it beautiful that we all got to do this together, after all?

Thank you Rachel Letofsky, for your persistence, patience and "cautious optimism."

Thank you to early readers and cheerleaders: Sara Quin, Erin Wunker, Andrea Warner, Daniel Zomparelli, Jonny Sun, Paige Sisley, Ron Eckel and Léonicka Valcius. I needed your wise feedback and kind enthusiasm more than I can express.

Thank you to the soundtrack dream team, James Bunton, Shamik Bilgi and Rachael Cantu for bringing these fictional songs to *life*.

Thank you, Suzette Mayr, whose sublime writing pushed me to make judicious word choices.

Thank you, Caleb Nault, for the job intel.

Thank you, Simon Underwood for once pointing out that my work seldom reflects my sense of humour — an excellent and difficult challenge.

Thank you, Manjit Thapp, for granting us permission to use your striking artwork as the cover, which helped me fall back in love again, and Jessica Albert for bringing it all together perfectly.

Thank you to all of the artists and academics mentioned in this book. I am ever inspired by and grateful for your words, images, sounds and ideas.

Lastly, thank you to the Canada Council for the Arts for your generous support — and more specifically to the members of the jury. Your decision gave me a vital boost and has changed my life.

At ECW Press, we want you to enjoy this book in whatever format you like, whenever you like. Leave your print book at home and take the eBook to go! Purchase the print edition and receive the eBook free. Just send an email to ebook@ecwpress.com and include:

Get the eBook free!*
*proof of purchase required

- the book title
- the name of the store where you purchased it
- your receipt number
- your preference of file type: PDF or ePub

A real person will respond to your email with your eBook attached. And thanks for supporting an independently owned Canadian publisher with your purchase!